The Mythical Blond

The Mason Braithwaite Paranormal
Mystery Series, book 9

Also in this series:

Praise for the series:

Mason is a hero like none who have come before him: a sensitive, queer P.I. whose only weapon is his intuition. This book turns the detective genre on its head and makes you think about the ninety percent of your brain you're not using.
—Teja Watson, author of *Attic.doc*

Every foray by Church's wonderful psychic detective Mason Braithwaite is a truly suspenseful page-turner in the most unusual crime series ever, and certainly one that no aficionado of crime fiction should miss.
—David Osborn, author of the best-selling thrillers *The French Decision* and *Love and Treason*

Thanks to Christopher Church for giving us another exciting and well written adventure with one of my new heroes.
—Amos Lassen

Another fast-paced ride through Los Angeles by Church, who continues to reinvent and reinvigorate Mason Braithwaite. Church's writing is vivid, the worlds he creates believable, and his characters have a breadth of humanity, strength, and vulnerability that makes the series a fun-filled, page-turning adventure.
—Jeremy Randolph, author of *The Mural*

The Mythical Blond

The Mythical Blond

Christopher Church

DAGMAR
MIURA
LOS ANGELES

Published by Dagmar Miura
Los Angeles
www.dagmarmiura.com

The Mythical Blond

This is a work of fiction. Names, characters, businesses, places, events, and incidents are either the products of the author's imagination or used in a fictitious manner. Any resemblance to actual persons, living or dead, or actual events is purely coincidental.

First published 2018

ISBN: 978-1-942267-73-7

prologue

Effie drove too fast on the dirt road back to the highway, rattling the car and jarring him to the bone, but Mason held his tongue, afraid of provoking her. He hoped the dust cloud rising from the tires didn't billow back toward Iris and spoil her lunch.

"I wonder if she's why we were supposed to stop?" Mason said as they pulled back onto the paved road. "She was the only human being for miles."

Effie scoffed. "She wasn't a human being at all. I thought you would have picked that up, Mr. Psychic Detective."

He stared at her. "What are you talking about? She was sitting right there, as real as you or me."

"All that jive about the dark canyon."

"What makes it jive? It's a great story. I actually want to do that hike someday. I should write down the name of that place."

Effie looked at him and frowned. "It's a great story because it's mythical. She's not real, Mason. She's a myth."

one

Oddly enough for a guy who made his living as a psychic, Mason was caught unawares by the strangers in dark suits, completely out of place among the reference shelves on a workaday Monday afternoon. He'd come downtown to the central library to read about how precognition worked. He'd never really believed it—his own insights were woolier, relating to hidden information rather than coming events. Lots of psychics claimed they could see the future, though, and he wanted to understand the ability. An array of reference books piled around him on the desk, he was engrossed in reading and scribbling highlights on a yellow notepad, not noticing the pair, a man and a woman, both in their early twenties, until they appeared in front of him.

"Are you the detective?" the man asked gruffly.

His partner glanced up from her phone screen. "Pasty redhead. That's him."

"Who are you?" Mason asked, startled. He sat back in his chair.

The woman held out a black wallet and deftly folded it open toward him. The ID card inside bore her photo with ARMED FORCES OF THE UNITED STATES emblazoned across the top. He managed to read her name, JOHNSON, M., before she pulled it back.

"We represent Lieutenant Ortiz of the Equipment Verification Command. His office would like to interview you."

"A lieutenant in the army?" Mason said, looking them over. They were dressed in street clothes and looked officious, but at least neither one of them was visibly armed, and an ID card didn't have the power of a badge.

"The Equipment Verification Command," the man said, enunciating carefully, as if he should have heard of it. "That's the Navy."

"What does your lieutenant want with me?"

"We don't have that information," the woman said, putting her hands on her hips. "We're here to arrange transport."

"I'm not going anywhere with you," Mason said, meeting her gaze.

"We're not here as an escort," she said, her tone authoritative now. "We're arranging an interview."

"You're not law enforcement, I know that much,"

Mason said, rising from his chair, his heart pounding, stuffing his notepad into his backpack. "So I know you can't arrest me." He pulled the bag onto his shoulder and turned away, headed toward the lobby.

"Mr. Braithwaite, hold on a minute," the woman called after him, but he ignored her. They didn't follow, he saw with relief when he glanced over his shoulder as he started up the stairs. The pair of them just stood there scowling and watched him go.

Apart from being intimidated, it felt weird to be approached like that, in a public place. Even though Johnson had flashed an ID, he wasn't convinced they were who they claimed to be. It was possible they were representing someone he already knew, someone from an old case. Maybe he could find out.

Logically, they wouldn't be hanging around the library for long. There were only three ways out of the building, and to access any of them, they would have to pass the same point, the checkout desk in the lobby. If he could see them leave, he might be able to follow them. He knew just the place to watch without being seen.

Across from the checkout desk was a video room, with shelves full of disks, separated from the lobby by glass walls. Even though Mason didn't easily blend into any crowd, towering over most people and with his shock of red hair, he could lurk among the videos and watch people coming and going. When he got to the lobby he ducked into the room and stood in front of a shelf, positioning himself so he could see beyond it toward the desk, where a few people waited to scan their books before leaving. He took a few deep breaths to calm down.

The suits could also leave through a staff door, or an emergency exit, he thought, eyeing the patrons walking by, mostly students at this time of day. But no—there they were, dressed to blend in but standing out, if you were tuned in to it, with their decisive gait, their officiousness, striding past the directory board toward the Hope Street exit. He flinched when he spotted them, instinctively pulling back, out of view, but as he'd suspected, they were no longer looking for him, and headed for the exit.

Waiting a few seconds, he followed, then paused in the doorway when he caught sight of them, trotting down the stairs to the street, one after the other. He stepped out and started down the stairs once he was sure they weren't going to look back. There were dozens of places to go down here—parking lots, the metro—but they walked up to either side of a white SUV parked brazenly at a red curb in the little dead-end street.

Maybe they really were military. Only cops and bureaucrats would have the nerve to do that, position a vehicle so illegally in a dense and busy commercial district; an ordinary person would return to find it towed away, facing steep fines and hours of effort to get it back. He trotted down the last set of steps as they climbed into the SUV and slammed the doors, and got close enough to read the license plate. The vehicle wasn't marked, but the plate bore the familiar blue U.S. GOVERNMENT label. He pulled out his phone and typed in the plate number as they drove away, oblivious that their target was standing on the sidewalk behind them.

He watched as the SUV turned into the traffic, headed west. Looking over his shoulder to make sure he wasn't being watched, which he knew was irrational, he set off for the metro. Trotting down the stairs into the station, he scanned the platform carefully before he ducked onto the train. He'd tangled with enough shady characters in this job that he should be used to it, but still, the encounter had rattled him.

If they were feds, he'd never heard of the agency they'd mentioned, or the person who wanted to see him. The only government type he'd run across in his work was a woman who worked for the NSA and had passed him some useful surveillance information on the Billy Blood case. At least he had assumed she was NSA; she'd never actually confirmed that. Were these military types after him because of her? He'd dealt with plenty of people with resources, crooked and otherwise, and he knew it was never safe to interfere with the interests of someone with power. Whatever it was about, he doubted that ditching them at the library was going to be the end of it.

It was just a few minutes' ride to his stop, in a gritty urban part of Los Angeles. Mason lingered on the platform before walking up the stairs to the street, scanning the other passengers, but the suits weren't among them, of course, and no one showed him any interest.

His bicycle was parked where he'd left it, in a rack

at the top of the stairs, and soon he was pedaling in his own hilly neighborhood, calmer with each turn on the winding route as the fear ebbed away, then up his own street, panting with the effort on the last half mile, despite the fact that he rode it almost every day.

Ned, his boyfriend, was home when he went into their hillside house, sitting in the living room drinking coffee with their friend Gilbert, the sunlight streaming in the French doors from the balcony. It was funny to see them sitting across from each other—although they'd grown up together and shared Latin heritage, they were visually opposites, Ned in a flawlessly ironed dress shirt, his hair natty and suave; Gilbert's mane wild and unkempt, his loud punk-band T-shirt and the torn knees in his jeans not a statement but more likely what he had lying around to wear that day.

Ned briefly held Mason's arm as he stooped to kiss him hello, effortlessly intimate, making Mason feel grounded without saying a word.

"Hey, Stretch," Gilbert greeted him from the sofa. "You're all out of breath."

"That hill isn't getting any easier," Mason said.

"Do you want a coffee?" Ned asked.

"Sure—I'll get it," Mason said, and stepped into the kitchen. Ned had used the *briki,* which he only ever did when Gilbert was around, so Greek coffee was a treat. He filled a demitasse cup and went back into the living room.

"Gilbert's staying for dinner," Ned said.

"Great," Mason said, standing there cradling his

little cup. "Let's catch up then. I need to do some work."

He went down the hall to the office he and Ned shared and sat at his desk, then pulled open his laptop. Typing in "Equipment Verification Command" as a web search, he sipped at his gritty coffee and scoured the results. It was a real entity, he found, part of the Navy and with no discernable connection to the NSA. The agency's website showed an eagle in profile superimposed on a rhythmically undulating rendition of the flag. The empty symbolism made him grin; it revealed nothing about the organization or its mandate, but like a defensive talisman, it precluded criticism—who would dare complain about a majestic eagle or the flag?

There were a few breezy paragraphs that mentioned quality control, adherence to ISO standards, and the agency's pride in its best-and-brightest staff, but it shed no light on what the Equipment Verification Command actually did. Its headquarters was described vaguely as "near Las Vegas, Nevada," but no address or military base were mentioned. Staring at the screen, he thought for a minute, trying to recall the name of the officer that the suits had mentioned. It was a lieutenant, he had retained that, but he couldn't remember the name. The suit's name was Johnson, he'd seen that on her ID, but being so common, it wasn't even worth searching for; there'd be hundreds of them involved in the military.

The one solid piece of evidence he had was the plate number. Digging online, he found the federal government was surprisingly forthcoming about its vehicle fleet, explaining that blocks of prefixes were assigned to specific departments, and after a few minutes he'd traced the number to the Bureau of Land Management. The plate he'd seen was supposed to be mounted on a BLM bucket truck in Wyoming. Maybe he'd written it down wrong, he thought fleetingly, but he knew that wasn't it. The Equipment Verification Command was starting to look underhanded.

He heard the front door close, and then a woman's voice, chatting with Ned and Gilbert. Their roommate, Peggy, was home from work. She stuck her head in the office a moment later and greeted him, her long brown hair still pinned up on her head, still wearing her dour gray work drag. Mason rarely saw her dressed for her day job, in a conservative law office, as she always shed the outfit as soon as she got home.

"Have you heard about dinner?" she asked.

"Not in detail."

"It's some kind of pizza that Gilbert wants. It sounds like it's going to be amazing."

"It always is," he said, grinning at her. She and Ned were both enthusiastic vegan cooks, and Mason ate well because of it.

Peggy waved and left, and Mason heard the door to her room click shut. It sounded like Ned and Gilbert had moved into the kitchen, and Mason briefly considered going out to offer to help with food prep, but he knew Ned didn't need it. He dug around some more for information about the Equipment

Verification Command, determining that it had nothing to do with the Bureau of Land Management, then got sidetracked reading his email and the news.

Eventually he heard Peggy go out to the kitchen, and the three of them talking. He folded his computer closed and went to join them. Peggy and Gilbert were sitting on stools at the counter that separated the kitchen from the main room. She had changed into slacks and a sweater, her hair down and casually tied back. Ned had his apron on, stained with red finger wipes, and was holding the oven door open a few inches and peering inside, but he closed it and came to the counter as Mason walked in.

"What's going on?" Mason asked.

"I was just telling these two I got some good news," Peggy said. "I got a permit to busk on the pedestrian mall in NoHo."

Ned leaned on the counter. "You actually need a permit?"

"They have to do it that way. If they didn't limit the number of performers, it would be chaos."

"It must have been hard to get," Gilbert said.

"Well, I had to audition. I figured it's a perfect venue for me because you can't use amplification."

"Are you going to perform as Peggy Pregnant?" Mason asked.

Her stage persona strummed an acoustic guitar and sang her earnest folk songs while wearing flower-child garb over an extreme baby bump, created with a strap-on faux belly she had found at a film-prop sale. The music was her own, authentic and sincere, and her fans never asked why she had been nine months' pregnant for so many years.

"Of course," she said. "I'm doing six to nine on Saturday night. Matt's coming."

"I bet you look great, even when you're pregnant," Gilbert said, with a wry louche grin.

"Why, thank you, Gilbert," she said, feigning pleasure. "You're such a gentleman."

"Will you make a lot of cash?" Ned asked.

She shook her head. "Other performers who've done it say you make like five bucks an hour. I'm doing it for the experience. It's a different way to connect with people than on stage. With passers-by you can see how they get drawn in by the music, how it affects them. Or so I'm told."

"We'll be there, right, sweets?" Ned said.

"I wouldn't miss it," Mason agreed.

Ned had him put out plates and cutlery, and soon he pulled his creation out of the oven, placing it carefully in the middle of the dining table. On top it appeared to be a pizza but it was at least two inches thick.

"It's beautiful," Mason said, sitting down with the others and pulling his chair closer. "What are we calling it?"

Ned grinned. "It's a pizza, but it's deep-dish style. A special request from Gilbert."

"I had it when I was in Chicago," Gilbert said, holding out his plate for Ned to serve him a slice. "This looks just like it. It even smells like real cheese."

"It is real," Ned said. "Made with cashews.

'Cheese' just means it's fermented, not what specifically gets fermented."

"What were you doing in Chicago?" Mason asked, passing his plate to Ned.

"I was at an experiencers' conference. It was quite enlightening."

"How is it going with your little gray friends?" Mason asked, eyeing him. Gilbert was regularly visited by extraterrestrials late at night, and Mason had recently helped him figure out how to cope with the phenomenon.

"It's happening less because I asked them to cool it. I'm still not sure why they want me, specifically, but a lot of people at the conference are in the same place. I have to say I'm happier with how things are going now."

"Good for you, man," Ned said. "You're getting on top of it."

"I couldn't have done it without your boyfriend," he said, and to Mason, "Have you seen them again? I was hoping they weren't going to get interested in you."

Mason shook his head. "No grays in my orbit. I did have a weird encounter with some of our own species today, though. Two government suits." He told them about the appearance of the duo at the library.

"What did they want from you?" Peggy asked, taking a bite of pizza.

"They said they didn't even know—they wanted me to talk to some lieutenant. No way was I going anywhere with them. I've been wracking my brain to find a connection, and all I can come up with is that NSA woman from the Billy Blood case."

Gilbert shook his head. "The Navy's totally different. The NSA might be shady, but whenever there's something extremely weird going on with the government, it's the Navy."

"What kind of weird?" Peggy asked.

Gilbert's eyes grew wide. "Aliens."

"How did they find you?" Ned asked Mason. "And why would they come to the library?"

"I go there a lot," Mason said.

"Still, I would think they'd look for you at your house."

"They can track anyone by cell phone," Gilbert said. "It's probably easier for them than knocking on your door, because you're always going to be where your phone is. If you don't have your phone turned on, their software can do facial recognition from security video feeds in real time. It's easy to follow you around—on the metro, or walking on the street downtown. They probably even knew what floor you were on in the library."

"I hate to think we live in that world," Peggy said.

Ned sighed, setting down his pizza crust. "Whether that's how they found you or not, we know such things are possible."

⁂

Gilbert left not long after dinner, and Peggy retired to her room. Mason helped Ned clean up, and was putting the last of the dishes into the dishwasher when his phone rang. He pulled it out and saw that the caller ID was "unknown." It was probably marketing. Curiosity got the better of him and he picked up, answering "Braithwaite."

"Mr. Braithwaite," a man's deep voice said. "I'm Lieutenant Clifford Ortiz."

"Lieutenant?" Mason said, feeling his heart start to pound. "Did you send your flunkies after me today?" Leaving Ned in the kitchen, he walked toward the office.

Ortiz laughed heartily. "I'm sorry we got off on the wrong foot. Can we video chat? I'd like to look you in the eye and explain about that."

"Sure," Mason said, and hung up, setting his phone on his desk while he scrabbled in a drawer for a notepad and a pen. His phone buzzed with the video call request, and he let it ring for a few seconds as he wrote "Lt. Clifford Ortiz" on his pad. He answered the call and propped the phone against his desk lamp.

"That's better," Ortiz said, grinning and leaning toward the camera.

Mason was startled at how good-looking he was—in his thirties, with a square jaw, his black hair in that idiosyncratic military buzz-cut. Just a few inches of his collar were visible, an open jacket with a dark-blue camouflage pattern. It made sense that he'd want to show his face, he thought; it was a strong asset. Mason dipped his head self-consciously so the camera wasn't aimed up his nostrils.

"So what's going on, Lieutenant Ortiz?" Mason asked.

"Military people are trained to get to the point," Ortiz said. "Cut through the fluff, state things clearly. When I put the word out that I'd like to talk to you, the gears of our big machine went to work, and I know that's not always pretty at the receiving end. They're sailors, not diplomats."

"They looked like spies, not sailors," Mason said.

Ortiz guffawed, his head tilting back. Mason hadn't been kidding, but it was disarming, he decided, that Ortiz thought that was funny.

"They didn't look like forest rangers either," Mason said. "The plates on the car they were driving were registered to the Bureau of Land Management in Wyoming."

Ortiz's eyebrows shot up. "You checked on that?"

"Like I said, they looked shady."

"I'm not sure what to tell you, except maybe that the federal government can be sloppy with the motor pool. I assume the plates were reassigned but the registration wasn't updated."

"OK," Mason said, frowning. "They said you wanted to interview me. Regarding what? Can we do it now?"

Ortiz leaned toward the camera, his expression earnest. "I do want to talk to you, but we should have framed it differently. I'd like to hire you."

"You want to pay me to talk to me?"

"Sure. We'd pay you for—" he paused, looking at something off to the side. "Your research insights.

That's your field, correct?"

"Technically I do psychic research, but yes, that's my field. Is this about something I've worked on before?"

"I can't really get into detail, but I assure you it's not about you personally. I'd like to talk in person if you're willing to come out here."

"Meaning somewhere near Las Vegas?"

Ortiz's eyes narrowed. "You really have done your homework."

Mason folded his arms. "I looked up your agency, and I still have no idea what it's supposed to be doing. It's awfully hard to trust you with absolutely no information."

"Mr. Braithwaite, it's the military. Thousands of ordinary people work for us. There's nothing to be afraid of." He grinned. "The food might be one exception. You won't find gourmet cuisine like you do in a big city like yours. Everyone complains about it."

"Don't overestimate the cities. There's lots of bad food in LA too." He sighed. "How would I get there?"

"We'll cover your travel and provide lodging," Ortiz said, businesslike once again. "We won't take more than two days of your time."

"That's pretty mysterious."

"No mystery," Ortiz said affably. "Just controlled information."

"I could use the work," Mason said, and picked up his phone, surreptitiously taking a screen shot of Ortiz.

"What are your contract rates?" Ortiz asked,

looking to the side again, "for your, uh, research work?"

"To travel out of town, I'd have to charge five grand per day." It was a ridiculous figure, ten times what he'd charge any client, but it was a calculated move—Mason wanted the inflated ask to provoke a reaction. It would help determine how serious Ortiz was about this.

"That works," he said simply. "There are some forms to fill out to get paid once you're here. Bring a government-issued ID."

"You're not going to negotiate? I thought that number would dissuade you."

Ortiz shrugged. "We buy pencils that cost more than that."

"If you can pay me that much, I'm in."

"Excellent," Ortiz said, nodding.

"When do you want me out there?"

"We'll book you on an early flight in the morning."

"Tomorrow?"

"Ideally, yes. Can you do that?"

"Yeah, I guess I can."

"I'll have someone send the details by email in the next few hours."

"Will someone meet me at the airport in Vegas?"

"Turn on your phone when you land at McCarran. We'll have more for you then."

"OK," Mason said.

"I'll see you tomorrow," Ortiz said, and ended the call.

Mason stared at the screen as it went black, parsing the conversation. Why hadn't Ortiz asked for an email address, or his legal name for the air ticket? The reason was obvious, but it made him uneasy: Ortiz already knew all those details. He already had Mason's phone number too, he realized, and somehow knew he'd be at the library. Hopefully it was all information gleaned from military-grade data collection, or even the kind of software that Gilbert had described, facial recognition that could find him on the metro, rather than targeted personal surveillance. He didn't want to slip into paranoia, but there might be good reason to.

After he spent a minute making notes about the call, he opened his laptop and did a web search for Ortiz. He wasn't the head of the Equipment Verification Command, but reassuringly, his name was listed in relation to it in several places, even though there was no indication of his job description or duties, and no photos of the man. Mason made some more notes and pulled a clean manila folder out of his bottom drawer. On the tab he wrote LIEUTENANT CLIFFORD ORTIZ—NAVY, and tore off the pages he'd written, stuffing them inside.

He was missing something, he thought, setting the folder open on his desktop and scanning his notes. Then it clicked: there was no ocean in Las Vegas. What was the Navy doing there? A quick web search revealed that there were two military bases near Vegas, Nellis and Creech, but both were Air Force. Scanning through a summary of each place, they seemed to deal with drones and bombing training, with no mention of the Navy.

More germane was the question of why Ortiz wanted him. The research job felt like an angle, a way to get him to cooperate. It had to be something about a previous case. His psychic insight had never misled him, so he spent a minute now tuning in to it. He closed his eyes and cleared his mind, pushing away the noise and random thoughts that came up, and gradually shifted his focus to the edge of his awareness. *Is meeting Ortiz a bad idea?* he wondered. *Should I bail on this?* No clear inspiration came, negative or otherwise, even though he sat there in his empty state of mind for quite a while. Finally he opened his eyes, not really sure whether no information equated to no risk.

His phone buzzed with an email, and he picked it up to check. The sender was a no-reply at a snarled string of numbers and letters with the ".mil" domain at the end, and the content was just an image attachment. Clicking it open, he saw that it was a boarding pass for a flight at seven tomorrow morning. They'd even spelled his name right. This was really happening.

Ned was already in bed, reading, when Mason went into their bedroom. He peeled off his clothes and climbed in.

"Who were you on the phone with?" Ned asked, setting down his tablet and sliding an arm around Mason's neck.

"The guy who sent those suits to the library. They

want to hire me for two days' work in Vegas."

"He just called you?"

"We actually had a video chat."

"Why do they want to hire you?"

"He said it was 'controlled information,' but I'm thinking it's about something I've already worked on. I looked him up, and it's legit—he's in the Navy."

Ned sighed. "I'd love to say I'm surprised that the military is hiring psychics, but sadly I'm not. My tax dollars at work."

"At least I'll be earning back some of those dollars. Can you drive me to LAX? I have to be there early, so you'll be back home before your work day starts."

"Sure. You're going to be tired, though."

"You have no idea." He rolled closer to Ned, nuzzling his shoulder. He was glad that Ned accepted that he wasn't a morning person. If only he were as accepting of the whole psychic thing.

"Why did this guy want to video chat?" Ned asked. "I never do that for work calls."

"I'm not sure. Maybe to build trust, so he's not just a voice on the phone."

"What does he look like?"

"The boy next door—if the boy next door were a supermodel."

"I wish you had a photo."

"I do," Mason said, and rolled toward his side of the bed to retrieve his phone from the night table. He pulled up the screen shot of Ortiz and handed it to Ned.

"I can see how he might be considered good-looking in some cultures."

Mason laughed. "If that guy lived next door, you'd sit on the porch to watch him work on his car, and bring him iced tea, and flirt with him shamelessly."

Ned handed the phone back and held his gaze. "Don't flirt with him," he said firmly.

"I'd never do that. You're so much hotter than that guy."

"Good answer," Ned said, and moved closer, kissing him hard.

He was initiating sex, Mason realized, and went with it, pulling Ned up on top of him, even though he had to be up so early.

Later, after he'd drifted off, in the dream world, Mason was walking along an arroyo of black sand and gravel. It was the desert, he knew, but the sand was unfamiliar, way too dark. Maybe it was volcanic—sometimes he saw blotches of that out in the Mojave. There were miniature drifts of dry snow in sheltered places, and bits of green growing here and there along the edges. It's cold here, he thought, the gravel crunching under his feet, and then realized he was dreaming. He thought about manipulating his surroundings, actively changing things to obtain some insight, but before he could focus on doing that, the environment evaporated, and he sank deeper into sleep.

two

Waking to his strident alarm, it felt like the middle of the night, reinforced by the darkness outside. The first gray glimmer of daylight had barely begun, the winter sun as reluctant to rise as he was. Killing the alarm, he sat up on the side of the bed so that he wouldn't drift off again. Ned was already up, audible in the kitchen. The floor felt cold to his feet, and it motivated him to get moving.

Ned had coffee and oatmeal waiting for him, and he gratefully tucked in, then threw together an overnight bag. There wasn't really enough stuff to merit a whole suitcase, he decided, with just a change of clothes and his toothbrush, so he folded everything into his backpack with a fresh blank notepad.

"Is that what you're wearing?" Ned asked when he came out of the bedroom.

"I can't really wear shorts. It's too cold in Vegas. I checked."

"I meant maybe something dressier than tan chinos and a plaid shirt. It's a work trip, right?"

"When I talked to him, the lieutenant was wearing camo. I don't think he'll care."

"Suit yourself," he said, and Mason followed him out to the garage. "We'll take the Crown Vic, I think." Both Ned's cars were classics that he kept in pristine condition with the help of his gearhead brothers. The sporty Barracuda was fun on a night out, but for an early-morning airport run, he was right, Mason thought, the sober Crown Vic made much more sense. Ned pulled it out of the garage and Mason climbed in the passenger seat, setting his backpack on the floor between his feet. Skillfully nosing the oversize car down the hill, Ned pulled onto the boulevard and navigated to the freeway. There was a surprising volume of traffic for such an early hour.

"I emailed you all the info I could find about this Navy guy," Mason said, "just in case there's anything hinky going on. I don't even know exactly where I'm going."

"I don't think you have to worry. If they wanted you for anything clandestine, you would have just disappeared off the street."

"That's not especially reassuring," Mason said, looking out over the sea of taillights.

Soon they were crawling along the roadways looping through the airport, and Ned deftly swung the Crown Vic up to the curb when they reached the right terminal.

"Call me," Ned said, and Mason kissed him good-bye and climbed out.

He bought another coffee once he was through security, sipping it as he walked along the terminal to find the gate. Once he'd boarded he found his seat, on the aisle, and had just settled in and buckled his seatbelt when a woman in the stream of shuffling passengers stopped beside him.

"Hey, you," she said, beaming at him. "We're going to be working together."

"Really?" Mason asked, looking her over. She wore a beige pantsuit, and her hair, or more likely a wig, he thought, was in stiff blond curls that made her look older than she was, probably in her late fifties. Her earrings were bright red plastic disks, more reminiscent of the buttons holding up a cartoon character's drawers than jewelry, and behind her trailed a purple child-size roller bag.

"Ma'am, can I help you find your seat?" the flight attendant called to her, annoyed. She was indeed blocking the narrow aisle, holding up the line of people behind her.

"I'd better go," she said, and patted Mason's shoulder, cheerfully adding, "See you in Vegas, baby," as she continued toward the back of the plane.

Mason craned around to watch her go, her lumpy brown handbag slung over one shoulder. It was as bulky as his backpack but looked a lot less comfortable.

How had she known him? Maybe she was a psychic, and Ortiz had hired her too. If that were the case, Ortiz had shared more information with her than with Mason. She found her seat and hoisted the purple roller bag up into the overhead bin, then caught Mason's eye and waved at him with a toothy smile. He held up a hand and turned away.

It was the second time in two days that a perfect stranger had recognized him. Surely things would be cleared up when he met Ortiz, but still, the thought of it made him feel queasy again. He needed to push that aside. *Weirdness is your business,* he reminded himself.

Vegas was so close to LA that the plane started descending not long after it was in the air. Walking out into the terminal, he didn't wait for the blond woman, but sought out a coffee place, switching on his phone as he waited in line. A text message popped up:

Please proceed to gate K-42.

In his mind, all along, Vegas had been his destination; he hadn't even considered that there might be a connecting flight. Only one boarding pass had been attached to that email. He slammed his espresso and headed toward the gate, several minutes' walk from where he'd arrived, at the quiet end of one arm of the terminal. The whole area was deserted, he saw, except for a lone woman behind a desk; either he was very late or this was the wrong place. But the door to the boarding ramp was open, although the woman wasn't wearing a uniform, an ID card on a lanyard around her neck the only indication that she worked here.

Approaching her, Mason said, "I think I'm supposed to be on this flight, but I don't have a boarding pass."

She smiled and asked, "Government-issued ID?"

Mason dug out his wallet and handed her his driver's license. She slid it through a reader and looked at her computer screen for a second.

"It's open seating," she said, handing his ID back and gesturing to the ramp.

Putting his wallet away, he asked, "So where is this flight headed?"

She raised an eyebrow. "You should know better than to ask."

"Right," Mason said, looking down the boarding ramp and hesitating for a moment. Once he went in, that was it—he was all in. This was the last opportunity to back out. But he didn't, squaring his shoulders and striding through the doorway.

It was a regular-size airplane, but only a dozen or so people were on board, scattered around the cabin. Some were in military fatigues, sandy gray and green rather than the blue camo that Ortiz had been wearing, but most were in civilian garb, dressed like office workers. Halfway back, seated at the window, he spotted a familiar blond head. She noticed him as he entered and waved at him wildly.

"Hey," she called to him. "Come and sit with me. Come on back here."

He could position himself on the aisle and leave a seat between them, he reasoned, as a buffer from her hyperactive enthusiasm. He walked down to join her, and she watched him, a broad smile on her face, as he set his backpack in the bin and got settled.

"Do you know what's going on?" he asked her quietly, leaning across the seat between them.

"No idea," she said, shrugging. "But when your Uncle Sam says jump, you jump. What's your name?"

"It's Mason."

She extended a drooping hand and said, "Effie."

He gave it a delicate shake. "I thought you already knew me. You recognized me on the LA flight."

"I had a flash of you and me sitting together on an airplane, and voilà, here we are. I recognized you from that. The red hair is hard to miss."

"So you're a psychic."

She tilted her head. "Well, I get glimmers, and I remember the future sometimes."

"Then you're a true psychic."

"I guess," Effie said, sounding uncertain.

"I was just reading about that. It's called precognition."

"I didn't know that was the name for it. To me it feels like déjà-vu, but for things that haven't happened yet, you know?"

"Do you work as a psychic?"

She laughed. "I work the desk at a hotel. I used to run an orchard in the hills in Ventura, but there's no money in that, and then with the drought, it was getting harder to produce anything at all. Then I got married, so there were two of us in the orchard, and twice as many mouths to feed."

Mason nodded, trying to absorb it all, feeling overwhelmed by her effusiveness. She was slightly built but muscular, which made sense if she was accustomed to the manual labor of a fruit farm. "Where's your hotel?"

"In Long Beach. My beloved husband and I live in San Pedro."

She pronounced it the Anglo way, Mason noticed, "*pee*-dro," the way the locals did, far from the original Spanish.

"Listen to me, babbling like a fishwife," she said, gently slapping Mason's arm. "You'd think I'd never been on an airplane before. Tell me about you—are you a psychic?"

"I am," he said, smiling at her banter. He pulled a dog-eared business card out his pants pocket and handed it to her.

She admired it for a moment, tapping the logo Peggy had designed for him, the sun and moon wrapped around the Eye of Horus.

"So mysterious," she said. "Just like the lieutenant. This is going to be fun."

"You were hired by Ortiz?"

She met his gaze. "I already have a job," she said slowly, as if he might have missed that, "in a hotel. Lieutenant Ortiz wanted to ask me some questions."

"About what?"

"Who knows?" she said, grinning blithely. "I'm assuming it's about some of the foreigners who stay at the hotel. A few of them would certainly be on the radar of the national security folks. There are some interesting characters, let me tell you. I don't gossip, but one time this Southeast Asian prince of some sort, his name escapes me"—she gestured vaguely—"Prince Something-or-Other—got arrested for meth. That guy could party. I didn't know there was that much Dom Perignon in the whole city. The police had to let him go, though, because he had a diplomatic passport."

"Did Ortiz tell you it was about that guy?"

"Not exactly," Effie said. "But it has to be something like that."

"So you just got on an airplane to another city without knowing why you were going?"

Her eyes grew wide. "Didn't you do the same thing?"

"Yeah, I guess I did," Mason said, his cheeks reddening. She was right—he was in no position to judge her.

"Show me your hand," she said, waggling her fingers. He reached toward her, but she said impatiently, "the other one." He switched hands, and she briefly held it, rubbing his knuckles. "No ring on that finger," she said, her expression one of mock concern. "You're not married?"

"No, but I've been with the same guy for several years."

"Five is the magic number," she said, patting his hand. "If you make it to five, it gets easier. I met my dear husband when I was in the fruit business." She locked eyes with him and said gravely, "We're very deeply in love."

"I see," Mason said, not daring to look away.

The plane pushed back and the flight attendants started a safety demonstration. The normalcy of watching it felt reassuring, that not every routine and convention of ordinary life had evaporated. Once they were airborne, a young man in military fatigues stopped and squatted in the aisle beside them.

"Ms. Brownstein, Mr. Braithwaite," he said, eyeing them both. It wasn't a question; he knew who they were. "Can I get your phones, please?"

"Can I just switch mine off?" Mason asked. "I'll put it in my backpack."

"No way," he said, and shook his head. "Military security."

Pulling it out of his pants, Mason powered it off and then handed it over.

"Any other electronics?" he asked, sliding the phone into his breast pocket. "Cameras, voice recorders?"

It took Effie a minute to find her phone, digging around in her purse, but once she'd surrendered it, the guy pocketed it with Mason's.

"I'll need to have a quick look in your bag," he said, and Effie handed it over, scowling but not protesting. He set it down on the empty seat across the aisle and dug through it, briefly examining her key ring, and carefully feeling the lining.

"Your bag, sir?" he asked, handing Effie's back to her.

"It's overhead," Mason said, and it was soon pulled open and pawed through, presumably to his satisfaction, as he stowed it again, and then did the same to Effie's roller bag, which looked to be full of clothes. When he was done he walked away without another word.

"I'm assuming we'll get those back," Effie said.

"We're descending again," Mason said, feeling the aircraft dip. "That's the shortest flight I've ever been on."

Peering out the window, he could see a flat and lifeless stretch of brilliant white rising to meet the plane. Desert salt pans weren't uncommon in the Southwest, and some of them occasionally filled with water, but many of them hadn't been wet for eons, the white minerals shining perpetually in the bright sun. It was an ideal place to build an airport, he realized, as it was already perfectly flat. In the distance he glimpsed a water tower, some squat utilitarian structures, and aircraft hangars, all with Nevada's endless mountains rising in the distance.

After touching down the plane came to a halt near a cluster of buildings that looked nothing like an airport terminal. The door was opened and the few passengers aboard started filing out, tramping down a wheeled metal staircase onto the tarmac. Squinting in the bright daylight, Mason followed Effie down the steep steps, keeping one hand on the railing. The sun felt warm through the sharply dry morning air. It was the desert climate at its most hospitable, in the winter.

Waiting at the bottom was a familiar face. Ortiz

was tall, he saw; maybe as tall as Mason. Effie had obviously video-chatted with him too, because she approached him as the other passengers trooped past him toward the buildings beyond.

At the bottom of the stairs Mason glanced back at the plane, puzzled that it had no name or logo emblazoned on it, like they always did. There wasn't even a registration number, he realized—it was a completely blank airplane.

"It's so lovely to meet you," Effie gushed, touching Ortiz's arm. "Can I call you Cliff?"

Mason wondered fleetingly whether she was so effusive with everyone, or if it was magnified by the uniform and that handsome face.

"Usually it's 'Lieutenant,'" Ortiz said, "but for a pretty lady like you, we'll make an exception." He winked at Mason as Effie preened with delight. "Mr. Braithwaite," he continued, turning to Mason. "I'm glad you could join us."

"Call me Mason."

"Call *me* anytime," Effie said.

Ortiz laughed. "Now, Effie, what would your husband say?"

Effie playfully slapped his arm. "What he doesn't know won't hurt him."

"May I?" Ortiz said, gesturing to Effie's roller bag. She handed it to him and he set off with it trailing behind, leading them toward the rows of buildings.

The scream of jet engines suddenly filled the air, but Ortiz ignored it, not even looking up. Mason stopped to watch. At the horizon, still on the perfectly flat lake bed at the foot of the distant mountains, he could see gray delta-shaped wings shooting almost vertically into the air, impossibly fast, one set after another, four planes in all.

"So where are we?" Mason asked, catching up to Ortiz. "You said you're in the Navy, but this is the middle of the desert. There can't be any boats within a thousand miles."

"You're right about that. It's mostly an Air Force facility," Ortiz said. "It's called Groom Lake."

Mason looked back at the salt pan, at the far-off airplane tails wavering in the heat. "Area 51?" he demanded. "You brought me to Area 51?"

Ortiz gestured to the vast open space. "It's not what the conspiracy theorists think it is. When there's no official information provided, people make up stories to fill the empty space. But you'll find no flying saucers parked here. It's just an aircraft testing facility."

"What are we doing here?" Effie said, her gung-ho tone now tempered by doubt.

"We'll discuss that in a minute," he said, smiling reassuringly.

Once they were off the tarmac, which ended abruptly without a fence or any other demarcation, just the lip of pavement, Ortiz led them past several identical low-slung buildings, none of them signed, finally approaching one and pulling open a door. It was cooler inside, where they were joined by a woman wearing fatigues in the same blue camouflage pattern that Ortiz wore. She took Effie's bag when Ortiz handed it to her.

"Ms. Brownstein, I'm Petty Officer Patali. If you'll come with me," she said, looking at Effie.

"Sure. See you later, boys," she said cheerfully, waggling her fingers, and followed the woman down the hall.

Effie's escort was wearing a sidearm, which was a little unnerving, Mason thought, watching them go. But then again, this was a military base. Ortiz took Mason in the opposite direction and stepped through an open doorway into a dark room. It took a second for his eyes to adjust to the low light, but he could see there were a couple of chairs and a big window in one wall. He almost overlooked another man in fatigues standing in the shadows at the far end of the window, watching them as they entered. The view through the window wasn't to the outside but rather into an empty conference room with a long table and chairs, a podium and a video screen at one end.

"This is Petty Officer Khalif," Ortiz said.

"Hey," Mason said, glancing at him, but Khalif didn't reply, except for an almost imperceptible nod. It sounded like a Middle Eastern name, Mason thought, but Khalif looked African, maybe Somali.

Ortiz stood at the glass, and Mason joined him.

"What am I looking at?" Mason said, turning from the empty room to Ortiz.

Rather than answer, Ortiz nodded to the glass. In the conference room a door opened and a woman in an orange jumpsuit walked in, followed by another young woman in fatigues, her hair pulled back tightly. It wasn't Patali, but just like her, she was wearing a sidearm. The military woman glanced up at the window, but the woman in orange stood and stared straight ahead, her expression blank.

"Do you know her?" Ortiz asked, watching Mason's closely.

Mason's heart started to pound. He knew now what this trip was about. The woman in orange, her vacant eyes, dark complexion, ratty dry black hair—he recognized her instantly. Laura. He put his palm on the glass and tapped with his fingertip, but she didn't seem to hear.

"Why is she here?" Mason asked.

"Answer the question."

"I thought I was here to work, not to be interrogated."

Beyond the glass, Laura pulled out a chair and sat at the table. Her guard stood near the door, hands folded behind her back.

Ortiz sighed and stepped back from the glass. "Come with me," he said, and went back into the hallway. Khalif waited for Mason, then walked out behind him. Ortiz opened a door on the opposite side, a few steps farther down, and Mason followed him in. Khalif stood in the doorway. He was wearing a sidearm too, Mason saw.

"Have a seat," Ortiz said, and waited as Mason set down his backpack and dropped into a chair.

There were no windows here, just a small table with utilitarian chairs on either side, and with three of them in the confined room, it felt crowded. Even though he'd never been here before, it was familiar, almost a cultural archetype—this was an interview room; there was one in every police station. Ortiz stepped out and closed the door behind him, leaving Mason sitting alone in the claustrophobic little space. He didn't even need to try the door to know it was locked. Things had quickly taken a dark turn, he thought. This wasn't a job—it was a trap.

three

I t wasn't surprising that Laura was here, being held at a secretive military base. She was no ordinary person, but he couldn't believe she posed any threat to the government. Mason had met her out in the Mojave when she was on a paranormal cleanup job. He'd stumbled into the phenomenon she was investigating, and she'd helped him out of it, had literally saved his neck. If she needed his help now, he'd do whatever he could—but that didn't seem remotely plausible, given that he was just as much a captive as she was.

He could hear Ortiz and Khalif conferring outside the door, their voices too low to make out the words. The door opened again and both men stepped in, sinking into the chairs across from him. Ortiz smiled, still friendly, not at all like a cop about to drop the hammer.

"Am I under arrest?" Mason demanded, looking from one to the other.

Ortiz frowned. "Of course not. This is just a friendly conversation."

Mason scoffed. The guy could spin it however he wanted, but he knew he had the power to detain him indefinitely.

"Did you ever play football?" Ortiz asked, leaning back in his chair and lacing his fingers behind his head.

"Is that the one with the weird-shaped ball?"

Khalif chuckled.

"Not a sports fan, huh?" Ortiz said. "I just figured you're kind of built for it."

"Someone may have made me do it once in PE, but I must have blocked it out. I do admire their cute little outfits, though."

"OK, Mason, I get it. We're not going to bond over football."

Mason looked around the little room. "Is that what's going on? It feels more like you're gathering evidence."

Ortiz nodded, his face clouding, and moved his hands to the table. "When did you and that woman first meet?"

"'That woman'? Didn't she tell you her name? She's clearly a prisoner here; what does that have to do with me?"

"So you do know her. Where do you know her from?"

"If I answer that, are you going to put me in one of those orange jumpsuits? Is that the plan for me anyway, regardless of what I say? And what's wrong with your petty officer? He's awfully quiet."

Khalif raised his eyebrows. "That gives you the chance to speak. Most people relish the opportunity."

Mason could see that Ortiz's amicable facade was giving way to frustration.

"You've answered every question I've asked you with another question," Ortiz said. "I'm in the business of collecting intelligence, Mason, not distributing it."

"Is Effie being interrogated too?"

"Nobody's being interrogated," he said sharply. "She's next door, and she's a guest here, just like you are. Although she's being a lot more cooperative."

It was just a tactic, Mason knew, using social pressure to chide him into being more forthcoming.

"Your boss here has quite the mac with women," Mason said, turning to Khalif. "All he'd have to do is blow in her ear and she'd tell him anything you wanted."

Khalif guffawed, throwing his head back. "Well, I guess you have to use the tools you've got."

Ortiz shook his head and watched Mason, eyes bright, calculating. "Would it work on you?"

"Are you kidding me?" Mason said, louder than he'd planned. "I'm not saying anything else until I know why I'm here."

"You haven't really said anything at all." Ortiz sat back, frowning, but he seemed calm, bemused rather than angry.

It was a good sign, Mason thought, that neither one of them was upset. It made the situation feel much less sinister than it had a minute ago.

"Effie is a real spark," Ortiz said finally. "I don't think I could handle her, even if I was straight. I'm a man's man, like you."

"Oh, god," Mason said, tilting his head back and looking at the ceiling. "You would have to be, wouldn't you."

"What are you talking about?"

"It's like going into the doughnut shop," Mason said, waving his arms, "and you say, 'I can't eat any of these because nothing's vegan,' and then they tell you, 'No, man, everything's vegan, help yourself,' and that makes it worse, since you still can't eat anything, because you have healthier food waiting at home."

Ortiz's eyes narrowed. "I'm not sure I follow."

"You could get any man you want, Cliff, I'm certain of that. But it's not going to work on me. Just like the football buddy thing didn't work."

He folded his arms, mimicking Mason's posture. "You should be more cooperative if you want to get paid."

"Getting paid is the least of my concerns right now. That's how you lured me here, telling me it was a job, but nothing about this feels like work. I'll be happy if I even see daylight again. What about Effie? She said she wasn't working for you, so, what, you just appealed to her patriotism? That's low, man."

"You think I lured you here, like some kind of trick?" Ortiz scowled, color rising in his cheeks. "We protect this country, Mason. Have some respect."

"It's nothing personal. You're very charming, and you got me to come here of my own volition. Even Khalif seems pleasant, despite the fact that he's packing heat. But here we are, in a windowless room, two on one, and you're the one who gets to ask questions." He gestured at the closed door. "I get the feeling a lot of your interactions end up like this. I know you people have clandestine prisons, extrajudicial rendition, indefinite detention without charges, and lots and lots of secrets. Nothing about that is worthy of respect."

Ortiz's mouth tightened. "We're not the bad guys," he said, and stood, quickly followed by Khalif. They walked out, and Ortiz closed the door behind them.

Mason took a deep breath and ran his fingers through his hair, then slouched forward, his palms on his knees, to catch his breath. Maybe mouthing off was a mistake. Regardless, there was nothing to do now but wait.

They hadn't gone far—he could hear their muffled voices just outside in the hallway. Mason rose and stepped silently to the door, gently putting both palms on it and then pressing his ear to the surface.

"I'm not seeing any signs of deception," Khalif was saying.

"Maybe not, but we're also not getting any answers."

"It's difficult to start a narrative when we don't want to tell him what we know."

"I just wish he wasn't such a belligerent knucklehead," Ortiz said.

"Maybe you should just brief him."

"That's not how this works. We'll move on to the next phase."

Mason jumped away from the door and landed in his chair just as the door flew open again. Ortiz stood there, filling the frame, oblivious to Mason's fluster, grinning and breezy again like he'd been when he greeted them at the airplane. "Laura would like to talk to you."

Mason rose, startled, and followed him out into the hall. Khalif didn't accompany them as Ortiz led Mason around a corner and into the conference room he'd looked in on earlier. The wide window he'd stood at was an opaque reflective surface on this side, and there were several smaller mirrored panes in the other walls, probably for cameras, he realized, or for Khalif to watch. Ortiz stood near the guard, hands on his hips, and watched as Mason approached the table and pulled out a chair opposite Laura.

"Hello, Mason," Laura said, her expression blank, her eyes not quite looking at him.

"How are you?" he asked, sitting down and leaning toward her. He knew that Ortiz and probably an array of recording devices were listening intently, but he asked anyway: "Why are they holding you here?"

Laura smiled but didn't answer, still staring into space.

The sound of the door opening pulled his attention away from her vacant eyes. It was Effie, coming into the room and looking worried. The woman who'd escorted her earlier, Patali, wasn't with her. She walked around Mason's side of the table.

"Do you know her, Mason? Is she a prisoner? I told them I've never seen her before in my life. I've seen some crazy things over the years, but I don't know anything about any prisoners." Effie set her handbag on the table with a clunk and took the chair next to Mason. Ortiz sat down too, at the end of the conference table, near the door.

"Are you certain?" Ortiz asked Effie, tenting his fingers. "I thought all of you knew each other. These two certainly do."

"I already told your petty officer that I didn't," Effie snapped, glaring at him, with no trace of her earlier infatuation.

The door swung open again and a young man wearing a white kitchen jacket, a hairnet on his almost hairless head, came in with a tray and set it on the table near Ortiz. It was laden with muffins, bagels, and four paper cups of steaming liquid.

"I hope nobody wanted decaf," he said, glancing around the room.

"This is fine, thanks," Ortiz said, and the guy left. Ortiz took one of the cups and rose to slide the tray toward Effie and Mason. They each took a cup, and Mason took a bagel, grateful for the carbs. It was indeed coffee, he thought as he took a sip, but it was wartime-style, as thin as tea. Still, it was hot, and familiar, and made him feel a little less like a detainee.

Ortiz looked at Laura, his hands wrapped around his cup. "We brought your friends, Laura. Don't you have anything to say to them?"

Laura stared at the wall, showing no sign of having heard him.

"Did you drug her, Cliff?" Effie said, her eyes on Laura, her lip curled in distaste, absently peeling the paper from a muffin.

"It's not drugs," Mason said. "You won't be extracting any intelligence from her right now. Not in this state."

Ortiz's eyes narrowed, his face still a mask of friendly interest. "What state is that?"

"I'm not sure what you'd call it," Mason said. "Semi-catatonic, maybe?" He'd seen her like this before, spaced out, although he wasn't about to tell Ortiz that. Her mind was elsewhere, literally focused in another physical place or time, and what they were seeing was the delay in her focus, like an overtaxed computer. He knew she'd eventually come out of it.

"Laura, where did you meet these two?" Ortiz called to her.

"How many times do I have to say it?" Effie said to him, raising her voice. "I've never seen her before."

Laura turned to Effie and said simply, "I summoned you." Her face remained expressionless.

Effie stared at her, appalled.

"Maybe you can explain why," Ortiz said.

They waited in uncomfortable silence, all eyes on Laura. Finally she said, "Driving."

Effie leaned toward her. "They arrested you while you were driving? What were you driving, honey, a semi-trailer load of counterfeit Valium?"

Laura was still for a minute, but eventually she turned to look at Ortiz. "You should tell them. Things will progress more easily."

"Tell us what?" Effie demanded, looking at him too.

Ortiz hesitated, pursing his lips, glancing from Effie to Laura.

Mason looked at him expectantly. "After all, we're just having a friendly conversation here, Cliff."

"Fine," he said. "It's not classified." He sipped his coffee and leaned back in his chair. "Laura here was driving a beat-up little car on a backroad in the Mojave, and she lit up a radiation detector like it was World War III."

"Like an explosion?" Mason asked, incredulous.

"No, like nuclear material—like twenty pounds of cobalt 60. We sent out an entire unit to round her up."

"Why do you have radiation detectors on backroads in the desert?" Mason asked.

"Drones," Laura said flatly, staring at nothing.

"That *is* classified," Ortiz said, eyeing Laura. "The problem we have is that neither the vehicle nor your friend here are radioactive anymore. We've taken that car apart and gone over every inch of it, but the signal is gone."

"Clearly your detectors are broken," Effie said. "Plutonium doesn't just evaporate. Or maybe she threw it out of the car, and it's sitting out there by the side of the road, waiting for some bikers to find it, or a busload of kids on the way to camp."

"I never said it was plutonium," Ortiz said, frowning. "We picked up a gamma radiation signature. Our equipment is working fine, and there's nothing radioactive out there. So my question for you two is, what can you tell me about all this?"

Effie sighed and shook her head. "Cliff, you're pretty, but you don't seem all that smart." She glared at him and raised her voice. "I don't know her."

"Finally," Mason said, slapping the table, ignoring Effie. He leaned back in his chair and grinned at Ortiz. "Thanks for finally being honest. Sometimes that's all it takes, man."

Ortiz leaned forward, focused on Mason.

"I don't know anything about radiation," Mason continued, "but I know Laura. I met her in the Mojave near Los Angeles a while back. She was camping by my friend's rancho. We've met a few times, and she gave me a ride once, but we're not close." It was an honest answer, even though it omitted the paranormal details that would make it harder for Ortiz to believe.

Ortiz thumped the table, emulating Mason's gesture. "At last we're getting somewhere."

"Lieutenant, I haven't seen the sun for days," Laura said, suddenly lucid. "Could my friends and I take a stroll outside?"

Ortiz slumped back, surprised. "I'm sure we can arrange that. Give me a minute," he said, and rose, stepping out of the room.

"Who is she, Mason?" Effie asked him quietly, her eyes on Laura. "She looks foreign."

"She's not deaf. I'm pretty sure her ancestry is Native American, which makes her less foreign than you or me."

"But she's so weird."

"She's just a little preoccupied," Mason said. "Disconnected."

Laura grinned at her, meeting her eye, but didn't speak, and froze again. Ortiz came back a minute later with Patali.

"Follow me, the three of you," Patali said.

Mason stood and watched Laura, but she seemed present now, and rose from her chair. They followed Patali out of the room and through a doorway at the end of the hall into the daylight. Ortiz didn't accompany them, instead heading down the hall in the other direction.

It was already warmer, Mason noticed, squinting at the brightness, and it felt good to be outside. In the sky a blurred streak of gray was followed by the shriek of a jet engine, so fast that he only caught a glimpse of it before it was gone. Effie looked around for the source of the noise, but Patali ignored it. She must be used to it, Mason thought, if this place really was about testing aircraft.

They were in a dusty yard between the bland and functional buildings, no other people anywhere in sight, no fences, just sand and concrete and a couple of unmarked white vehicles parked next to doorways.

In the distance he could see a couple of arching airplane tails, much bigger than the fighter jets, just visible in an open hangar. It was easy to see why Ortiz was willing to let them go outside. They didn't need fences—there was nowhere to escape to.

Patali stood nearby, at the ready, not watching them directly but definitely within earshot.

Laura gave Mason a little hug, seemingly fully focused now, a smile on her face. "It's so good to see you," she said.

"You're actually here?" Mason asked, meeting her eye.

"Finally, right?" she said, and chuckled.

Mason glanced at Patali, who was clearly tuned in to their conversation. "Are you recording us, or just eavesdropping?"

Patali met his eye and frowned. "You're on a military base under armed guard. What do you think?"

"I've already been interrogated by you people. Nothing would surprise me."

"Oh, you haven't been interrogated," Laura said. "Not really. If the military wants something out of you, they can give you drugs, deprive you of sleep, hypnotize you. It's all perfectly legal too."

Mason lowered his voice to speak to her, even though he knew nothing he said was private. "What are you doing here?"

Laura shrugged. "Things happen." She looked out at the yard. "Let's move away from the building."

Mason strolled with her, Effie following, with Patali hanging back a little but not far behind.

"You seem awfully nonchalant for a prisoner," Effie said.

"I'm not really a prisoner. I can leave any time I want."

Effie gave Laura's orange jumpsuit the once-over. "How can you just leave?"

"Mason knows."

Effie looked at him expectantly.

"Not really," Mason said, shrugging. "I'm only aware of the broad strokes."

"As another version of myself," Laura told her, "I can influence individuals within the military command structure." Her hands danced in the air, moving invisible blocks around. "That's one thing about military people—they do what they're told from the higher levels without a lot of backtalk."

"What other version of yourself? What are you talking about?" Effie demanded.

"I thought I'd use the opportunity to do some research here," Laura said, turning away from her.

"You're researching this place?" Mason asked. "Ortiz said it's just an aircraft testing site. There aren't any saucers."

"He said that?" Laura said, raising her eyebrows. "Well, it must be true, then."

"What's here?" Effie said, stepping closer. "Have you seen saucers?"

"Not personally, but I've seen some interesting tech. A stealth aircraft with high-voltage electricity on the leading edge of the wings, for example. I'm not sure why they're doing that. Don't touch the airplanes—you'll fry," she said, grinning at them. "Also, there's aliens."

"What?" Effie said, alarmed. "Where?"

"In the new part of the base." She gestured to the taller slate-blue buildings in the distance. "There are saucers in the hangars, and extraterrestrials working in the underground areas. I think it's some kind of collaborative project."

"We should watch what we say," Mason said, eyeing Patali. "We're being monitored."

"You mean our gracious escort Petty Officer Patali, or the parabolic mike on the roof over there?" Laura said. "Either way, it won't matter. I'll see to that."

Patali shot her a look but didn't say anything. She looked concerned, not offended, Mason thought. He scanned the rooftops around the yard, squinting to locate the microphone, but he couldn't see it.

"Don't worry about finding it. It doesn't matter," Laura said. She linked arms with him and turned her face toward the sun, eyes closed, enjoying the bright light. "There's nothing quite like the winter sun."

"I want to hear more about the aliens," Effie said. "What do they look like?"

"I had Ortiz bring you both here for a reason," Laura said, still facing the sky. "Effie knows why."

Mason glanced at Effie. Her expression had changed.

"I wondered about that," she said quietly.

"What did you do?" Mason asked. If it had attracted Laura's attention, it was definitely problematic.

Effie looked away, embarrassed. "It's hard to explain."

"Not that hard," Laura said, turning to her. And to Mason, "Have you heard of energy avatars? Casting out virtual versions of yourself? They're usually generated by intent focus, sometimes in the dream state."

"I actually read a book about them," Mason said, "although the author didn't call them that. She called them projections. I did a job in a haunted building, and at first I thought that phenomenon was the explanation for the haunting. It's about focusing on another place, right? You concentrate on the idea of your childhood home, and then the people who live there today see you walking around it like a ghost."

"It's more than just thinking about something. It involves strong emotional focus. But you're right, the avatars are sometimes interpreted as ghosts. Usually those versions of you return when you break focus, or they get diluted, like jet-engine vapor dispersing in the sky."

Mason glanced up, but there were no contrails visible in the vast blue expanse. The screaming fighter jets seemed to be on a break. Looking at Patali, she was watching them intently now, but she looked baffled.

"At most they are weak echoes of the original projection," Laura continued. "That's why ghosts are fleeting and ephemeral. It takes a lot of energy to be in two places at once."

"Don't you do that a lot?" Mason asked.

"Not energy avatars. I have physical counterparts in various times and places, and we're all connected.

They're not projections—they're as real as I am. My thing requires a lot more focus. I'm not always fully here-and-now."

"I'm keenly aware of that," Mason said. "What do energy avatar projections have to do with Effie?"

"Tell him," Laura said to her.

"Well," Effie said, not meeting his gaze, "Something like that did happen to me recently. I was thinking about the old days, the time when I ran the orchard. I was feeling kind of nostalgic, you know?"

"I know how nostalgia feels, yes," Mason said, trying not to sound impatient. Laura briefly put her hand on his back, a tacit admonishment.

"So I went up to Ojai and went into the orchard, among the trees I know so well. The new owners weren't around. They don't live anywhere near there. I was thinking about all the years I'd worked that land."

"More than thinking," Laura said.

"Right. I was intently focused, as you said. I sat against a tree and surveyed the landscape. It was beautiful, and the sun was going down. I was looking at the shape of the branches, the trees. I knew it all so well. Everything was the way it used to be." She had a faraway look in her eye, her embarrassment forgotten. "I was remembering the fruit harvest, the good years and the bad years. And then I could see more. It was almost like I was seeing inside the trees, seeing their essence."

"You were tuned in to them through their lives," Laura said. "Seeing their entire life span."

"Is that what it was?" she said, still gazing dreamily

into the distance. "It certainly was unusual. I'd kind of anticipated it earlier in the day, like I knew that it was going to happen. Something powerful."

"Your déjà-vu thing," Mason said.

She nodded, meeting his eye. "Right. I got lost in the experience, loving on those trees. The whole orchard seemed alive, vibrant."

"Lots of people do that when their minds wander," Laura said. "They send parts of themselves off to a place or a time. But somehow you opened up a whole bunch of points at once."

Mason frowned. "You mean points in time?"

"Exactly. It's like she stepped into the lobby of an office building and looked at the directory, and suddenly there's a copy of her in every room in the building all at once."

"I don't know how I did that," Effie said.

"You weren't aware of your potential," Laura said simply. "You were feeling such intense emotions. Your homesickness. You didn't hesitate to push it out as far as you could."

Still squinting in the bright morning light, Mason looked at Effie with new respect. On the surface she didn't seem like such a powerful psychic.

"So why did you get us to come out here?" he asked Laura.

"Your thought form didn't dissipate," she said to Effie. "It's smeared through time, filling that place, and spilling beyond it. It's acting like an interference field, like an oil spill on the sea, spreading farther and farther."

"I didn't know what I was doing," Effie wailed.

"I know," Laura said, stepping closer and putting a hand on her shoulder. "But you need to undo it."

"How am I supposed to do that?"

"I don't know," Laura said, dropping her hand. "I'm just here to tell you it's a problem."

"Is that why I'm here?" Mason asked. "To help sort this out?"

"In a way," Laura said. "Most important, I want you to drive my car back to LA and deliver it to Hanh."

"That's it?" Mason demanded, feeling the color rise to his face. "I'm the valet? I don't even like driving."

"You're getting paid for this excursion, are you not?"

Mason took a breath. "Theoretically."

"Right. And the ancillary reason you're here is indeed about your psychic skills. I thought you might be able to help Effie figure out what to do, if she rides back with you. You can talk it through, and maybe propose some solutions."

"That sounds like a long drive," Effie said dubiously. "It was easier on the airplanes. Maybe we could have a chat here before you leave with the car, and I can fly back."

"My instinct was to get you both here at the same time," Laura said. "It's as if you're intertwined. The implication is that Mason is part of your answer."

That was new, Mason thought: he was being asked for his input. He regretted snapping at her, now that he knew there was more to it than shuttling her car around. Over the years Laura and Hanh had mentored him in a hands-off way, but being asked for his own ideas was definitely a step forward.

"I appreciate the opportunity to contribute," he said, "but I wonder if I'm capable of fixing something like this. I'm not pan-dimensional like you are, able to manipulate reality from afar." He held his hands out and waggled his fingers like a puppeteer. "And I've never done what Effie's done. Don't you have a solution already?"

"I don't know everything. This is how it fits together right now," Laura said. She grinned, mimicking his gesture by holding up her hands plugging two invisible components together.

"OK … I'm willing to try," he said, not sure he was really up to it. "I wish I understood exactly what it was that she did."

"Do you want to go have a look?"

"You mean now?"

"We'll do a quick bleed-through," Laura said. "Just our conscious minds. Our bodies will stay right here."

"OK," he said, "but I haven't done a whole lot of bleed-throughs. It always takes me quite a while to make it happen."

"I've had more practice. Effie, we'll only be gone for a minute or two. If your friend in uniform over there gets bothered, talk to her about something."

"Sure," Effie said, but she looked worried, glancing at Patali.

Laura turned away from Patali and said to Mason,

"Put your hand on my shoulder."

He turned to stand beside her, trying to look nonchalant, and rested his palm on the rough orange cotton.

"Close your eyes," Laura said, "and don't let go of me until we get back."

Mason murmured assent and instantly felt the daylight drop away. He opened his eyes and found they were indeed in a new place, with steep hillsides around, covered with brown rock and scrubby brush—the California countryside.

"Oh, yeah, this looks like Ojai," he said. "You're good."

They were in the orchard, between rows of massive gnarled trees, casting the long deep shadows of the end of the day.

"She's over there," Laura said softly.

Mason followed her gaze, and sure enough, there was Effie, in a pink track suit, wandering among the trees. She was smiling, and tears shone in her eyes.

"She doesn't see us?" he asked under his breath.

"We're not really here," Laura said.

She was right, he thought. It seemed so real; he'd forgotten that. If he looked closely at the ground, he could still sense the dusty earth of the military base, the desert winter sun tucked one layer behind the tree branches and the evening sky. But exploring the phenomenon wasn't the point of this excursion.

Focusing on Effie, he watched as she sat down under a tree, leaning against it. He wondered if there would be any visual effect from her psychic oil spill, but it was already happening. The trees started to shimmer, as if there were multiple copies of them all stacked together, overlaid, with slight differences visible, the trunks within the trunks getting thinner and fading toward nothing, ephemeral apples hanging among the leaves. Effie seemed brighter too, despite the fading daylight. She was almost glowing.

"Can you tune in to her emotional state?" Laura asked.

"How?"

"Think about what she's feeling, and you should be able to feel it. Just for a second, though. Don't get swept away in it."

He watched Effie, concentrating, and Laura was right, he could feel it. As soon as he thought about it, opened that door, it flooded in, his heart swelling with a wave of sadness, and pride, and love.

"Oh," he gasped, his knees weakening.

"Let go of it."

He had to struggle to get away, to mentally shift focus.

"See what's happening to the trees?" Laura said.

He was rattled by the tidal wave of her feelings, but when he looked around, he could see that Effie's glow was suffusing the orchard. Billowing outward, the trees were getting lighter, the grass brighter, painted with her emotional intensity.

"I can see a visual effect," he said. "What's actually happening?"

"Look at how much energy she's throwing out. And it's multiplying. She's like a fusion reactor, and

I don't know where it's coming from. She's the one Ortiz should have pulled off the highway, not me."

As Mason watched, more variation became noticeable in the trees. They seemed to be moving faster, revving up, leaves and fruit flickering into existence and then gone again, strobing. It was surreal, and mesmerizing.

"You get the idea?" Laura asked.

"I think so."

"Close your eyes."

The bright light came back, and he opened his eyes again, blinking in the sun, surrounded by the desert and the dusty military base. He stood for a minute, breathing heavily, dispersing the rush of adrenaline.

"Your palm is a bit sweaty," Laura said, almost apologetic.

"Sorry," he said, and pulled it away. He'd forgotten he was holding on to her.

"What did you see?" Effie asked, concern in her voice.

"You, sitting in your orchard," Mason said.

"I already told you that part," she said flatly.

"You were wearing a pink track suit."

Effie's eyes grew wide. "You did see me. Did you figure out what to do?"

"It was just a glimpse of how it happened," Mason said.

"That's a good start," Laura said. "You two should definitely go together. Road trip! It'll be fun."

"It's fine with me," Mason said. "It sounds like

I'll be driving back regardless."

"I hate the idea," Effie said. "Absolutely hate it. Peeing in filthy truck-stop latrines. But I guess we can make the best of it. That last plane ride was super short, so we're not far from Vegas, right? That means it can't be more than five or six hours back to LA by car. We can share the driving."

"And talk," Laura said.

Effie grinned. "I'm pretty good at that."

Mason nodded. "That's the spirit." In truth he wasn't looking forward to it either, and him figuring out how to help Effie didn't seem likely no matter how much she talked. But he trusted Laura's judgment.

"Do you want to stay the night, or head out today?" Laura asked, looking from one to the other.

Effie glanced at Patali, then looked at Laura. "That's up to you?"

"We can arrange it however we want," Laura said. "Another version of me will tell Ortiz's department head what to do as soon as we decide."

"What, you just flip a switch?" Effie said.

Laura scowled. "Other versions of me have done the groundwork, days ago, months ago, days from now, positioning themselves to have just the right influence. Make a strategic phone call, send an email, delete a recording. I can't make these people do something random, but there's a specific pattern to what's happening with us, here and now, a thread running through reality. It took a lot of preparation."

"I get it," Effie said. "Sorry I asked."

"Let's head out today," Mason said. "Soon—there's

lots of daylight left. That way it won't be too late when we get home."

"Fine by me," Effie said. "The 15 will be a nightmare regardless. It always is."

"I'll start the process," Laura said. She looked at Patali, who was now thoroughly confused, fear creeping into her eyes. At least her weapon was still holstered, Mason thought. Patali took a few cautious steps to the side, leaving Laura frozen, lost in thought, staring at the place Patali had occupied a moment earlier.

Mason turned away; he'd seen this before. Looking beyond the aircraft hangars toward the distant mountains, the heat shimmered silver on the perfectly flat lakebed. He could see a shiny jumble of antennas at one end, their stalks painted red and yellow. Radio antennas were everywhere, so it wasn't odd to see them here, but why were there so many of them all clumped together? This really was a strange place.

The door they'd come out of earlier flew open and Ortiz strode into the yard, eyeing them as he approached. He stopped in front of them, hands on his hips.

"One of you must have some powerful friends."

four

Ortiz was flushed, perspiration beading on his forehead, as if he'd been exercising.

"What are you talking about, Cliff?" Effie said, moving closer to him. But Mason knew—Laura's machinations were in play.

"I've been ordered to release the vehicle to Mason and to send you two on your way. The official word is that there's no evidence there was ever any radioactive material. Up the ladder it's being written off as equipment error, even though I'm certain that's not the case."

"What about Laura?" Mason asked.

"She'll be our guest a little longer, I'm afraid," Ortiz said, glancing at her. Laura nodded affably.

"You seem upset, Cliff," Effie said, gingerly touching her blond curls, "but I'm relieved. The desert is way too dry for my hair."

Ortiz scoffed and shook his head, not masking his disgust. "This whole thing has been a cluster-fuck from the get-go."

"Ooh, language!" Effie said, her eyes bright. She wasn't offended, Mason thought, instead impressed, exhilarated at Ortiz's passion.

"At least you know she's not a radioactive smuggler," Mason said. "That has to be good news."

"I suppose it is. But it's not satisfying at all." He glanced at his watch. "There's a flight out to McCarran at 5:30, but I don't know how you're going to take the car. It's in a thousand pieces."

"Are you sure?" Laura said. "Maybe it's been repaired."

"No way. I'd know."

"Maybe you could check," she said, smiling sweetly. "It's important."

Ortiz glared at her, and hesitated, but then stepped away, pulling out his phone.

"Did you arrange for that too?" Mason asked her quietly.

"No need. It reassembles itself."

He shot her a sidelong glance, but she wasn't kidding.

Ortiz returned a minute later, clearly angry. "How did you know they'd done that?"

Laura shrugged. "Just a hunch."

"One of the crews must have done it. I don't know

why they'd bother, and I certainly didn't see the order. I can't understand it. It would have taken a week."

"Daylight's wasting," Mason said. "We should get on the road."

"You're going to drive?" Ortiz said, surprised.

"Unless that's not possible. There's a road back to Vegas, isn't there?"

"Yeah, there's a road," he said, and sighed. "Give me a minute and I'll have someone look over the car, make sure it's roadworthy."

"Before you do that, how do I get paid?" Mason asked. "Can you cut me a check before we go?"

"He's paying you to be here?" Effie said, incredulous.

"I'm working," Mason said irritably.

"I thought getting paid was the least of your worries," Ortiz said.

"The situation has changed. A deal's a deal, man. I would hate to think the military would scam me out of a day's wages."

"Come with me, both of you," he said. "Patali, take charge of Laura."

"I guess this is good-bye," Mason said, turning to Laura. "How can I contact you if I come up with a solution for Effie?"

"Take it to Hanh, like the car," she said.

"Will I see you anytime soon?"

She smiled and gave him a brief hug. "That's a relative term. We will indeed meet again." Turning to Effie, she tapped her temple and said, "Don't forget what we talked about."

Mason felt a twinge of guilt leaving her there in the dust with an armed guard, looking incarcerated in that forlorn shade of orange. But she was far from helpless, he reminded himself.

Ortiz led them through the maze of blocky buildings and Quonsets to an office with a long counter. Like many of the structures they'd passed it was functional and worn, everything about it looking like it had been here since the 1940s. A clerk quickly rose from his desk when he caught sight of Ortiz, who spoke to him briefly and then walked out. The clerk dug in a file cabinet and then eyed Mason, waving him over. There were two forms to fill out, which the clerk explained perfunctorily before handing him a pen and returning to his desk. No place was immune to bureaucracy, Mason thought, even a secret base in the middle of nowhere.

"How much are they paying you?" Effie called to him. She was sitting in a chair near the door, legs crossed primly.

"Not much," he said, and called the clerk back.

After he'd checked through what Mason had written, he said, "Payment is issued by mail in four to six weeks. The check stub will indicate the Equipment Verification Command."

"Sweet," Mason said.

Ortiz came back for them a few minutes later. "The car's drivable, I'm told," he said, and led them back between the buildings.

Mason recognized the vehicle as soon as he set eyes on it, parked on a roadway behind a white SUV.

If it wasn't Hanh's thirty-year-old beater, it was a close copy—the same shape and color, the same density of scratches and dents, the same perfectly clear windows. Ortiz went to the SUV to talk to the driver, and Mason walked up to the car. The hatchback was open, and his backpack had been placed inside, along with Effie's handbag and the little purple suitcase. He'd forgotten about those; they'd left them in the conference room. One thing didn't match Hanh's car, though—below the trunk he saw that it bore a Nevada plate, the blue lettering legible through the caked-on dust.

"We're going to drive this thing across the empty desert?" Effie asked, taking it in.

"I know this car," Mason said. "It'll be fine."

"If you say so," she said, but she didn't sound convinced. "I'm glad they remembered my suitcase. I wonder if I should change? What should one wear for a desert road trip?"

"Uh—"

"How about for waiting for Triple-A in a broken-down car on the side of the road for four hours?" she continued. "I have a cute little sun dress. What do you think, Mason, slacks or skirt? Am I going to have to help change a tire?"

"It's just going to be you and me and the open road," Mason said, exasperated at her banter. "I don't care what you wear. Do what makes you comfortable."

"It's going to be a long drive." She looked thoughtful. "Let's stick with the pants," she said, and grabbed her handbag before slamming the hatchback closed.

Ortiz turned to them and tossed something underhand at Mason, a jumbled whirl that flew toward him in a gentle arc, glinting in the sun. He caught it awkwardly against his chest, almost dropping it.

"Not a sports guy, remember?" Mason said pointedly. Examining it, he found a lone car key on a ring, attached to a fob with a cartoonish rubber bird. It had a big yellow bill—a pelican.

"Follow the vehicle ahead of you to the gate," Ortiz said, his tone businesslike. "They'll get you on the highway."

Mason nodded. "Thanks. It's been interesting, lieutenant. Nothing personal, but I hope I never see you again."

"I certainly can't say that," Effie said. "I could look at that sweet face all day." She stepped up to Ortiz and wrapped her hands around his ears, leaning up to give him a quick kiss on the mouth.

Ortiz grabbed her shoulders and pushed her off, looking flustered.

Mason couldn't help but laugh. "You reap what you sow, sweet cheeks."

Ortiz scowled at him, dazed. "If you break down, wait with the car. There's not much traffic on that highway, but somebody will stop."

"Will do," Mason said, and climbed into the driver's seat. Effie got in too, and he turned the key in the ignition, inadvertently squeezing the rubber pelican, which let out a shrill little squeak. The engine started up, sounding small and tinny, more like a lawnmower or a leaf blower than an automobile, but it purred smoothly, not missing a beat, perfectly healthy and in tune. The instrument panel came to life. There was no tach, just the speedometer and a coolant gauge, and the gas was on three-quarters.

The SUV in front started to pull away, and Mason slipped the car into gear. As soon as he lifted his foot off the brake, Ortiz turned on his heel and walked away.

"Good-bye, Cliff," Effie shouted out the driver's window, leaning across Mason's lap. Ortiz raised an open hand in the air but didn't look back.

"He seems upset," Mason said, rolling up his window and accelerating a little to catch up to the SUV.

"Of course he is," she said. "We won."

"It's not a competition," Mason said, looking at her quizzically.

"For men like him, it's always a competition."

Mason thought about that. "I guess I feel a bit bad for him. He has no idea what's really going on."

"I'm not sure I do either," Effie muttered.

Half watching the road, Mason explored the car's controls, pressing buttons and twisting knobs. He pulled out the ashtray, not sure what it was at first, sliding it all the way out of its slot.

"Damn it," he said, looking back to the road as the lead vehicle picked up speed. At least the tray was empty.

"This thing is an antique," Effie said. "When is the last time you were in a car with an ashtray?"

"My boyfriend has two classic cars, so it's a familiar feature to me. There's a trick to getting it out and back in again, though. It's detachable because you have to be able to dump it, but there's a latch so that it won't spill when you pull it out to use it."

"You seem to have bypassed that particular security measure," Effie said, and took the tray from his hand. "Watch the road. We'll worry about it later."

The car was peppy and responsive, Mason thought, even though the engine sounded like it was straining when he accelerated or went up the gentle rises on the undulating road. It was beautiful fresh pavement, but had no lane markings, probably by design. The SUV in front didn't drive as fast as the road would have allowed, keeping the pace sedate. Glancing in the rearview mirror, he saw another white SUV, identical to the one in front. It hung back several car lengths, not trying to pass them. It was the other half of their escort, Mason realized.

They'd been winding through the empty landscape for quite a while when Effie said, "It seems like a lot of space just for testing airplanes."

"It provides ideal privacy, though, to work unseen. If there's aliens in the basement, who knows what else they're doing out here?"

Effie snorted, and they rode in silence.

"This looks like new glass," she said finally, turning to look into the backseat. "All the windows are. Why would she have put new glass in such an old car?"

"I think there's other stuff going on. It looks like a car, but it's something more than that. She said it reassembled itself."

"Yeah, I wondered about that."

The car in front was slowing, and they came to a green gate stretching across the road. There was no guardhouse or turnpike, just the barrier at the end of the pavement and a dirt road continuing beyond. It wouldn't have been out of place on any desert ranch except for the trio of security cameras mounted on tall poles, and several large signs facing the other direction, mounted on the gate and on both sides of the road beyond. This must be the back entrance.

The SUV pulled to one side and parked. In the rearview mirror Mason watched as the other vehicle came up behind them, slowing to a stop. The driver of the SUV in front, wearing sand-colored fatigues and mirrored sunglasses, climbed out and walked back to Mason's side of the car. He passed two bottles of water through the window, and then handed him their cell phones.

"When you get back to pavement, turn right for Vegas."

"Thanks, man," Mason said, slipping his phone into his shirt pocket.

The gate swung open and the driver stepped back, waving them forward. Mason pulled around the SUV and slowed to a crawl as he drove off the pavement, gingerly rolling onto the earthen surface and not speeding up until he was confident it wasn't too washboarded. Receding in the rearview, he saw the gate was shut again, the twin vehicles parked there, watching them leave.

It was only a few minutes' drive to the paved highway, properly marked with a yellow striped line, and Mason eased the car up onto the smooth empty expanse. He could feel the tension in his shoulders melting, and a smile spread across his face when they passed a black-and-white state highway sign.

"We're free," he said.

"It's good to be out of that place." Effie looked at her phone and fiddled with it for a minute. "No service. I want to talk to my Elmer." In a pouty little girl's voice she added, "I miss my shnuggle bunny."

Mason glanced at her. "It might be a while. We're still in the middle of nowhere. That's why they put their secret base here."

"Give it some gas, at least," she said. "This isn't a dirt track anymore."

"I'm already way over the speed limit," he protested.

"So how do you really know that woman? What kind of magic was she pulling on Cliff?"

"It's not magic. She explained it—she exists in different places, and all of her selves share information."

"I know the multiple instances thing is possible," Effie said. "I think it's kind of what I did, what got me in Dutch with her. Still, it doesn't explain how she could manipulate Ortiz's orders in real time."

"She's not limited to the present moment. She's in contact with her selves working yesterday, or last week. It must get very confusing. No wonder she spaces out like that."

"That's so far beyond what I assume is possible," she said, gazing out the window. After a minute she asked quietly, "Is she an alien?"

"I had the same thought once. She told me that she wasn't. She said she was as human as I am."

"She knew about aliens, though," Effie said darkly.

"So what are we going to do about your leftover thought form?"

"I have no idea how to fix that," Effie said, her voice rising. "I can't go and talk to myself before that day, like Laura can."

"How did you do it? I saw you sitting there, looking upset."

"Not upset. Nostalgic, and maybe homesick."

The words she used to describe it didn't really matter, Mason thought. He'd felt it, experienced the emotions, knew the intensity of it.

"When I saw it coming earlier in the day—my déjà-vu—I didn't really get that it was going to be a problem. As it was happening, even, I didn't expect it."

"What did it feel like?" he asked.

She considered that. "You know when you have a balloon, and when it's flaccid it's the size of your thumb. Then you fill it from the helium tank and it blows up into this huge uncontrollable ball that wants to get away from you. It becomes a completely different thing."

"I understand the image," Mason said, glancing over at her.

"The orchard was like that—just an ordinary memory, a longing, and then it expanded." She cast her hands outward toward the windshield.

"I think I saw that effect," he said, and waited for her to continue.

"I kind of shifted my energy out in all directions, let it fill up the new space. I could even feel that it had some permanence, like a life of its own. I didn't think it mattered, or I wouldn't have done it. Does that make any sense?"

"Sure." He nodded. "Does reflecting on it give you any insight?"

She sighed, staring out at the desert rolling past. "If you're asking if I can fix it, I can't even begin to fathom a solution."

"I might be able to come up with something," he said. "And maybe Hanh will have some ideas."

"That's who you're taking Laura's car to?"

"I'm pretty sure this is Hanh's car. At least I've seen her drive it. She's a colleague of Laura's, and she's deeply immersed in the paranormal."

"I'd be happy to get any kind of help. Right now I'm at a loss."

They rode without talking for a while, rolling through the endless desert, only rarely passing an oncoming vehicle.

"Do you mind if I nap?" Effie said. "I was up with the birds." She scrabbled around for the controls and dropped the seat back until it was almost flat, then curled up with her back to Mason.

It was an easy drive on the nearly empty road, and he was actually enjoying it, lost in his thoughts, running through the events of the day. Forty minutes later he was jolted from his reverie when Effie snapped awake and sat bolt upright.

"Take the next left."

"Why?" he asked, glancing over as she cranked her seat upright. There was no sign of any side roads here, just the ribbon of highway.

"I saw it," she insisted. "I saw that we're going to turn. We're supposed to."

"Are you sure you're not just manipulating the future by telling me what to do?"

"I saw a sign that said 'Lazica,'" she said, and spelled it for him. "It's something about the next left."

"Is it far?"

"How should I know?"

The car crested a rise, and on the road ahead a brown highway sign came into view. Mason felt his heartbeat accelerate when they were close enough to read it:

LAZICA PICNIC AREA

¼ MILE

The arrow on the sign pointed left.

"Impressive," he said, and started to slow the car.

Effie jabbed her finger at the windshield, excitedly pointing out the side road. "Turn there. It's right there."

"I can see it." He grinned and turned onto the dirt path, taking it slow, the washboard surface rattling the car. It was just a few minutes to the end of the road, where it made a loop back on itself near some dusty picnic tables. There was no shade, although it was a pretty spot, with rocky hills rising to a ridgeline beyond the end of the road. The place was deserted save for a lone dark-red SUV.

"Excellent," Effie said as Mason pulled up and shifted into park.

"What now?" he asked, surveying the desolate scene.

"I didn't see anything beyond us coming here. But let's stretch our legs." She climbed out and slammed the door.

He got out as well and arched his back. It was warmer again, probably the warmest part of the day, and thin bands of striated clouds had moved in high above. Effie had walked over by the picnic tables and was intently doing some exercises, counting quietly to herself and rhythmically bending to touch her toes, first with one hand and then the other. It reminded him of the kind of workout program he'd seen hawked on late-night TV.

A bit of movement caught his eye on the nearby hillside. Someone was up there, walking on a trail that he could just make out, a thread in the landscape. She was slowly descending toward them.

"That's probably the owner of the car," he said, and sat on one of the picnic tables.

It was a colorful sight: the woman wore a pastel blue and purple jacket, green pants, and a pink day pack. Once she was within earshot, the hiker shouted "Hello" to them, and Mason raised an arm in greeting. Effie took a break from her workout and retrieved her water bottle from the car. As the hiker approached, Mason saw she had blond highlights in her close-cropped black hair. She'd never get lost in the backcountry with all that color.

"Were you on the trail?" the hiker asked cheerfully.

"No," Mason said, "but it's a beautiful day for a hike."

"Superb," she agreed. "The weather's perfect, and it's really pretty around here. Are you having your lunch? That's what I'm about to do."

"We're just taking a break from the road," Effie said.

"Do you want some apples?" she asked. "I stopped at a farmers market and bought a whole bag."

"I'd love an apple. That's very generous," Mason said.

The woman grinned and went toward her car. It chirped as she unlocked it and opened the rear door, pulling out a mesh bag bulging with fruit.

"Are they organic?" Effie asked as she brought them back to the table.

"They are—grown on a small farm in the San Gabriel Mountains."

"I'll have to see them," Effie said, eyeing the bag.

The woman grinned and dusted off the bench with her palm, then swung a leg over and sat.

Mason slid off the table and sat across from her. She handed him an apple, perfectly shaped and firm, a leaf still clinging to the stem. It was clean and shiny, and didn't even need to be polished. He took a big bite. It was delicious.

The hiker offered one to Effie, who took it and sat with them. She took a dainty bite and chewed slowly, savoring it. "Not bad," she said. "I used to grow fruit. This is a solid seven out of ten."

"It's actually amazing," Mason said. "I'd rate it a full ten." He took another bite.

"That's because you're used to factory-farmed food," Effie said. "This is in a whole other category."

"Thanks for this," he said to the hiker. "I'm loving it."

"I'm glad," she said, after she'd swallowed her own bite. "I'm Iris."

Mason introduced himself, and Effie too. "How long were you out there?" he asked.

"I went pretty far today. I'd heard about this box canyon, about eight miles in, with the ruins of an old homestead."

"Did you find it?"

Iris nodded, pausing to chew another mouthful of apple. "The canyon is deep and narrow, so the sun hardly ever reaches the bottom. There are long shadows, like it's twilight all the time. The canyon walls are dark. It's maybe some kind of volcanic rock, and the sand is black because of it. It's such an eerie place. There's no wind at all."

"You saw the homestead?" he asked.

"It had burned down, so it was just a charred ruin, with some rusted metal relics, broken adobe, ancient shards of glass. The only signs of life were some introduced plants growing along the arroyo. Poppies, I think. It must have rained recently because the arroyo looked like it had been running, and there was standing water in places."

"It sounds beautiful," Mason said. "There were poppies?" He didn't know much about horticulture, but he'd done plenty of hiking in the Mojave, and he knew it was unlikely that garden flowers would be growing wild in the desert, even in a wet spot.

"I think so. They're pretty distinctive."

Effie set down the core of her apple and snorted. "Was he there?"

Iris looked confused. "Who?"

Effie didn't answer, but raised her eyebrows expectantly.

Iris looked uncomfortable and shifted on the bench, looking to Mason. "So where are you two headed today? You're not really dressed for a desert vacation."

"I'm helping Effie work on some stuff," Mason said, "and returning a friend's car. We're headed to Vegas, then LA." He gestured to the bag of apples. "May I?"

She smiled. "Of course."

Effie shot him a look. Did she think he was being piggy? Maybe it was a warning not to say too much. He bit into another apple, savoring the flavor and texture.

"You're Angelenos," Iris said. "Me too."

"What part of town do you live in?" Mason asked.

"By the water."

"I'm north of downtown," Mason said, glancing at Effie, "and Effie's all about the South Bay."

"Nice," Iris said. "I'm in the biz. My boss is a producer."

"Doesn't he have any work for you this week?" Effie said, folding her arms.

Iris shot her a thin smile. "Nope. You know how film production is—hectic for a while and then dead."

"We should probably go," Mason said, eyeing Effie. She'd acted strangely enough on the military base, but this was something else.

Iris reached in her pocket and handed each of them a business card. It bore just two lines: IRIS YI and her email address.

"Thanks," Mason said, slipping it into his shirt pocket.

"Do you have a card?" Iris asked him.

"Right—right," he said, and dug into his pants, producing it a moment later.

"Psychic investigator. Interesting job title," she said, reading it. "Have you been on any reality series?"

Mason frowned. "I'm not an entertainer. I just do research."

"I see," she said, and pocketed the card. "Well, I'll call you if I ever need that kind of help."

Effie stood. "Do you want me to drive for a while?"

"That would be great," he said, and rose, handing her the keys.

They said good-bye to Iris, who had pulled out a sandwich, spreading the wrapper on the picnic table as an impromptu placemat, and went back to the car. Mason waved to her as they pulled out, and Iris waved back, food in hand.

Effie drove too fast on the dirt road back to the highway, rattling the car and jarring him to the bone, but Mason held his tongue, afraid of provoking her. He hoped the dust cloud rising from the tires didn't billow back on Iris and spoil her lunch.

"I wonder if she's why we were supposed to stop?" he said as they pulled back onto the paved road. "She was the only human being for miles."

Effie scoffed. "She wasn't a human being at all. I thought you would have picked that up, Mr. Psychic Detective."

He stared at her. "What are you talking about? She was sitting right there, as real as you or me."

"All that jive about the dark canyon."

"What makes it jive? It's a great story. I actually want to do that hike someday. I should write down the name of that place."

Effie looked at him and frowned. "It's a great story because it's mythical. She's not real, Mason. She's a myth."

"Maybe you should have a sip of water. I think you're dehydrated."

"I'm not talking nonsense. Look it up on your phone. Iris visiting the dark valley. It happened three thousand years ago, not this afternoon."

Mason pulled out his phone and powered it on. "Still no service." He looked at Effie, then out at the landscape flashing by. She was driving way too fast. "Maybe the story sounds like a folktale, I'll give you that. Maybe it's not a real canyon, and she made up some parts of it. So she has a vivid imagination. That doesn't mean she's not real."

"Oh, I'm sure the canyon was there, and I'm sure she found it. Didn't you see the way she was dressed? She's reenacting the visit to Hypnos, god of sleep. He lives in a dark valley, perpetually in shadow, just like this woman described. He grew poppies, just like her homesteaders."

"The poppies did strike me as improbable," Mason said. He thought about it. "That's why you asked her if he was there. You were talking about Hypnos. If he's just an allegory for sleep, not a real person, why would you ask about him?"

"She was the one spinning the allegories, not me."

"I don't think she understood what you meant."

"Maybe she didn't, or maybe she's just playing dumb. Maybe she just had a nap out there, and that was her symbolic connection with Hypnos. Either way, she's a mythological projection, or a symbol, or something like that. Like me, polluting the orchard with my overzealous projection."

It was an unusual idea, and surprising, coming from Effie, when she claimed not to be especially aware of the workings of the world beyond the everyday. When he'd first caught sight of Iris walking down the trail, he wondered if she might be schizophrenic—other people he'd known with the condition loved bright colors, wore too much makeup. But maybe Effie was the unbalanced one.

He couldn't dismiss it, though, he knew that much. Strange things happened all the time, and maybe Effie's take was just different than his. But he was certain that Iris was physically real, not some hallucination. Feeling in his shirt pocket, he pulled out her business card and glanced at it. She was most definitely real.

five

They rode quietly, Mason mentally going over what he'd experienced on the bleed-through to the orchard, until Effie interrupted his thoughts.

"Do you remember how much gas there was when we started out?"

"It was on three-quarters."

"Great," she said flatly. "It's still on three-quarters. The gauge is broken. We'll have to stop as soon as we hit civilization."

"I'm not so sure it'll need gas."

"What kind of car doesn't need gas? This isn't exactly an electric roadster."

"A car that's not a car. Not really. I think we're just

seeing a car because that's what it wants us to see."

She looked over at him, eyes narrowing. "And you think my Iris story is crazy."

"I never said that." He gestured to the console. "Did you put the ashtray back in?"

"I put it down and never touched it again."

"Neither did I, but it's back where I found it."

Effie stared at it, the black plastic facing flush with the rest of the dashboard. "You're sure you didn't do that?"

"Look at the windows. You said it yourself: how can the glass be so clear and clean? It's not really a thirty-year-old car."

She sighed and stared out at the road ahead. "I guess I have to keep an open mind."

"I will if you will," he said.

Before long they passed a highway junction, and Mason noticed there were a lot more cars on the road. He tried his phone again, and found that he was connected to the network. He looked up Iris and Hypnos, reading through the tale with amazement.

"I found the story you're talking about," he said. "It is remarkable how similar it is."

"Of course it is. It's the same story."

Mason scanned through another version on a different page. "In mythology Iris is the personification of the rainbow, and a messenger for the gods. She visits Hypnos to ask him a favor for her boss, Hera." He read from the page:

> The home of Hypnos is in a dark valley where the sun's rays never penetrate, his house perpetually wrapped

in shadows. Chamomile, lavender, and poppies grow nearby. Iris came in her colorful raiment, illuminating the house, rousing the old god from his slumber.

"It's almost the same description," he said.

"That has to be Ovid's telling."

Mason scrolled down and checked. "You're right, it's from Ovid. How did you know?"

"Only a Roman would include all those flowery details. The Greeks were more austere."

Mason looked at her, impressed. "You know your classics."

"Everyone should. It's the foundation of Western civilization." She gestured to the floor at his feet. "Hand me my purse."

Unwilling to put the heavy bag in her hand while she was driving at highway speed, he set it on the center console between them, on top of the parking brake. She dug around, mostly keeping her eyes on the road, eventually pulling out her phone and swiping at it, intermittently glancing down and then back at the road. Mason was about to offer to help when she held it up to her ear.

"Hey, pumpkin," she said, breaking into a smile. "I'm on my way home.... Yes ... Military people are so efficient. You know, chop-chop, no nonsense...."

Mason couldn't hear the other side of the conversation, but he was glad in a way that Effie wasn't divulging all the details of their day.

"We're driving, so maybe five hours.... A new friend. He's from Los Angeles too, and has wheels...." She asked him about his day and spoke a little longer, then made kissing noises. "Mwah! I wub oo."

Mason grinned to himself and realized he should text his own partner.

> Successful trip. Leaving Nevada early. Home later this evening. Won't need a ride.

He considered adding "I wub oo," but he knew it would only elicit a question mark in response, and then the humor would be eclipsed by the requisite lengthy explanation.

They seemed to have driven into a town, or maybe even a Vegas suburb. Effie slowed down and pulled into a gas station.

"You're sure it doesn't need gas?"

"Not if the needle hasn't moved."

"It hasn't," she said, and drove past the pumps to park in front of the store. "But if we run out of gas, you're the one who's going to be walking the white line, buster. I'm going to powder my nose. Could you get me a coffee and a Danish?"

Mason followed her into the store and bought two coffees and some snacks. After he put them in the car, he went back inside to use the men's room. When he came out, Effie was standing by the passenger's door.

"Can you drive?" she asked.

"Sure."

She threw the keys over the roof to him, and he grabbed them out of the air, the little pelican squeaking sharply, as if startled. Mason got his coffee cup nestled in a convenient spot and then got back on the highway.

"I don't think I could make it all the way through Vegas without my subconscious taking over and driving us to a casino," she said.

Mason laughed. "You're a gambler?"

"I like to have fun. That's what this town is all about. It makes me sad to be here without stopping. Any interest in spending an hour or two at the slots?" she asked hopefully.

He looked over at her. "I'd rather drive straight through."

"Yeah, that's probably for the best. It's not the time for fun."

Soon they were on the freeway, then passing the towering gaudy casino hotels of the Strip. Effie sat and nibbled her Danish, looking glum.

"Four and a half hours from here to my front door," she announced. "That's without traffic. Unless you continue to drive like my grandmother."

"I'll try to keep up with everyone else."

Once they were past the city and in the desert again, Effie said, "I hate this freeway. It means you're leaving Vegas."

"It's also the road *to* Vegas, though. It goes both ways, so doesn't that balance it out?"

"No—that's a completely different road, a completely different feeling, a different time of day."

Mason looked at her. "It's right there," he said, pointing to the northbound lanes.

"Exactly," she insisted. "A different view, a different experience. Nothing to do with this road. Look at all the traffic on that side. Everybody's coming from

LA. Imagine what that road would look like to you, how you'd feel. You'd be anticipating pure fun. This road is just the opposite—the way back to reality."

Reality was preferable to spendy Vegas any day, he thought, and once they passed the road sign telling them they'd crossed the border, he instantly felt lighter, even though he didn't know this place, the bizarre landscape paved with mirrors aimed at a solar power plant. It was more about knowing he was in California, knowing he was home. They watched the sun setting as they traversed a steep mountain range. Mason flipped down the visor and could see better, but the sun's glare seemed to make the traffic more sluggish.

"I need a pit stop," Effie announced, and Mason exited at the next gas station. While he waited for her he bought another coffee and some bananas, then went outside to lean on the car.

"Can I get you a coffee?" Mason asked.

"Not unless you want to stop six more times before we get home," she said. "But it seems to have put you in a good mood."

"It just tastes better because it's in California."

"That's totally irrational and chauvinistic. You know that, right?"

He laughed. "I'm sure you're probably right."

"I get the feeling that your friend's car feels the same way," she said, her tone suddenly subdued.

"Why do you say that?" he said, pulling open the driver's door.

Effie just stood on the curb at the front of the

vehicle. "Did you notice the license plates when we first got in the car?"

"I did."

"Check them out now."

Mason stepped to the front and looked at the bumper. It took a minute to register, but then it struck him. He was staring at a completely familiar thirty-year-old plate design, and it was covered in dust, as it had been this morning, but it was a California plate. Gawking at it, he stood there, a banana peel dangling from his hand. He stepped around to the back of the car, but the plate was the same, a dusty California tag where there had been a Nevada tag a few hours ago. His rational mind told him he was remembering it wrong, wanted to gloss it over, push it away, forget about it. But it really had changed, he knew that, struggling to retain the idea.

"That's the most direct evidence yet," he said quietly, "about what's really going on with this car."

"It's like one of those stick insects that looks like a twig," Effie said, still staring at the front plate. "It blends into its environment to go unnoticed."

Pulling himself away from it and ditching his banana peel in a trash bin, he climbed into the car with Effie. Back on the freeway, they didn't talk about it, although Mason knew she was thinking about it as much as he was. The psychic insights he usually had were much more nebulous, not the kind of experiences that generated artifacts in the physical world. It shouldn't really be surprising, but it was just so blatant, so tangible.

"I have an idea about undoing your incident," Mason said finally. "Have you ever done a séance?"

"No, but what possible good could that do? I don't need to talk to anyone who's dead."

"That's not what they're really for. It's a way to gather information from the hidden part of the world—we could tap into it and see if we can find a solution. Theoretically I think it's about coordinating the psychic power of several people so they can do more than an individual could."

"You've done it before?" she asked, looking over at him in the low light.

"Sure. I once helped conjure a guy who was lost."

"You just pulled him into the room from somewhere else?"

"We did. We were all high-level psychics, and it was hard work, but it's a powerful tool."

"That stretches credulity." She sighed. "How many people do you need?"

"I'm not sure, but at least three."

"Elmer would be up for it, I'm sure," she said. "Maybe the three of us could try."

"Great," Mason said.

"Not tonight, though. You and I are both going to be dog tired. When Elmer and I have been separated for this long, I know our evening will be consumed with the pursuit of carnal pleasure."

"OK," Mason said, mentally scrambling not to imagine that.

"I'm going to try to sleep again," Effie said, cranking her seat back down. "Take the 710. It's faster than the 110."

"We'll worry about that once we're in town."

"I know how to get to my own house," she said irritably.

"I've no doubt."

Yawning and sipping his coffee to stay alert, Mason negotiated the heavy traffic, reduced to stop-and-go speeds at times. Every time an additional lane appeared as they got closer to the metropolis, the traffic volume correspondingly increased.

Thinking about the little car, he wondered what it really was. A pan-dimensional object, like Laura? A living thing? He would ask Hanh, but he doubted he'd get a straight answer. If it could change its appearance and reassemble itself, maybe it could drive itself, he reasoned. Silicon Valley had been hyping that utopian pipe dream for years. The traffic was fluid, and he didn't have anyone in the lane beside him, so he let go of the wheel. The car gradually started to drift toward the white line, and he corrected its trajectory when he felt the warning grooves rumbling under the tires. Enough of that experiment, he decided, and soon enough he had to focus on negotiating the unfamiliar winding road down through the Cajon Pass.

"Where are we?" Effie said, sitting up and cranking her seat up again.

"In town. On the 210."

"I did it," she said happily. "Take the 605."

Mason frowned. "Actually, *I* did it. You slept."

"You know what I mean. The planning and every-thing."

Mason laughed. "I couldn't have done it without you, Effie. Put your address in my phone. It'll route us around the traffic."

"That's probably smart," she said, taking it from his hand and tapping the screen. "Computers can navigate so much more calmly than me. Elmer says I'm a complete harpy in the car. When I give bad directions, his face turns into this monster face, and he absolutely shrieks at me. It's the most terrifying thing you've ever seen."

Mason glanced at her, raising an eyebrow. "You should try using your phone to navigate."

She set the phone on the console so Mason could see it, and within the hour they were pulling up at her building.

"You have to come in and meet Elmer," she said.

"If I can use your bathroom, I'd love to meet Elmer."

She directed him to a parking spot, and Mason pulled her little suitcase out of the back, towing it behind him as she opened the door to the lobby. He followed her into the elevator, where she pressed the button for 11. She was glowing with excitement as they rode up, Mason thought, actually panting in anticipation. She stepped off ahead of him and hur-ried to her front door, twisting her key and bursting in. By the time Mason got to the door, she was all over Elmer, kissing him and writhing in his arms. From what he could see, Elmer was shorter than

Effie, gray-haired, and had a pot belly.

He wanted to look away, embarrassed by the raw passion, but he squinted and watched for a second as Effie smeared her lipstick all over Elmer's face. Closing the front door, he poked around and found the bathroom, in the small apartment's only hallway.

When he came back, Effie had mostly detached from Elmer.

"Where are my manners?" she said. "Elmer, this is Mason."

"Elmer Brownstein," he said, and firmly shook Mason's hand, looking him in the eye.

His dialect sounded Northeastern, Mason thought, and judging by that handshake, he had to be in sales, or maybe PR.

"Nice to meet you," Mason said.

"Thank you so much for taking care of my precious gem," Elmer said. "I can't believe you drove all the way back. That Navy guy said you'd be there a couple of days. What happened?"

"It's a long story, and it's confidential, dear one," Effie said, and kissed him. They got distracted in each other again, so Mason stepped over to the sliding doors, looking out at the balcony.

"I love your bamboo," he said. "What's growing in the smaller pots?"

"Herbs," Elmer said, pronouncing it *"hoibs."*

Definitely a New Yorker, Mason thought.

Elmer extracted himself from Effie's embrace. "I have a bit of a green thumb."

"You must have a great view from up here."

"In the daytime you can see the water. That's the black void out there. Effie and I," he said, turning back to her, "are going to be seeing a lot more water for the next little while."

Effie's eyes grew wide. "Why, dear heart?"

"Because you, pretty lady," he said, his voice rising like a showman, "are going on a cruise to Cabo."

Effie screamed and jumped up and down. "Why, dearest, why?"

"We're going to renew our wedding vows."

Effie shrieked and jumped, throwing her arms around him.

Mason couldn't help but laugh, caught up in the excitement. "Just like on TV," he said. "How long have you been married?"

"Two perfect years," Elmer said, turning toward him.

"OK," Mason said, nodding. "Wow." He'd assumed it had been a lot longer.

"After I talked to you today, I bought last-minute tickets. We sail Friday," he told her, and to Mason, "We can practically walk to the cruise-ship terminal from here."

"Congrats," Mason said, and to Effie, "Will you have time to do our séance before you leave?"

"I almost forgot," she said, her eyes growing wide.

"You're having a séance?" Elmer asked.

"Mason is a full-time psychic," she explained. "He's going to help me with some things, and you have to help too."

"Sounds like fun," Elmer said agreeably. "Maybe

we can ask Amelia Earhart exactly what happened to her."

"That's not how it works, dear one," she said, and to Mason, "Can we do it Thursday night? We'll be all packed and ready by then."

"That works for me," Mason said. "Should we do it here?"

"All we need is a table to sit at, right?" She gestured to the little round table in the kitchen. "Will that work?"

"Perfect," he said, and nodded. "Well, I guess I should be going."

"My dear, it's been a slice," Effie said, giving him a tight hug but mercifully not kissing him the way she had Ortiz. "Thanks for all the driving."

"She drove too," he said to Elmer over her shoulder.

"Did I give you my number?" Effie asked him. "Call us when you're on your way over Thursday. And we should have dinner some night after we get back from Cabo."

Mason pulled out his phone and typed as she recited her phone number.

"Or bridge," Elmer said. "Do you play bridge, Mason?"

"I don't. Is it hard to learn?"

"Very," he said.

Mason grinned. "See you Thursday," he said, pulling open the door and walking back to the elevator. On the ride down he marveled at the pair of them. So passionate, and so expressive, bordering on irrational. If he greeted Ned that way after eight hours apart, Ned would have him hospitalized.

When he climbed into the car, he made a phone call.

"Pretty Nail Blowout," the receptionist answered.

"Is Hanh available?" Mason asked.

"She's not in, but she should be here tomorrow."

"What time do you close?"

"Nine p.m."

"Great," he said, and checked the time. That was over an hour from now; he should be able to make it.

It was well before nine when he pulled into the parking lot of the Sunset Boulevard strip mall that was home to Hanh's nail salon. He took his bag out of the back, slinging it on his shoulder, and then pulled open the shop's door, to be greeted by the familiar receptionist.

"I brought Hanh's car back," he said.

"OK, thank you," she said, as if she'd been expecting him.

"Is it OK to leave it here overnight?"

"No problem," she said, and took the keys. She squeezed the rubber pelican, making it squeak. "So cute," she said.

"It is, isn't it?" He turned back to the door.

"Thank you. See you soon," she called after him as he went out into the night.

The bus on Sunset arrived promptly, barely giving him a chance to nod off while he waited on the bench. Back in his own neighborhood, walking up the hill felt good, a little exercise after a long day of sitting.

When he got in, the house was quiet and empty, but Ned had left a note:

Gone to a meeting. Your dinner is in the oven.

He smiled and pulled out the meal, grabbed a fork, and sat at the counter to eat. AA kept Ned sane, but even with that to focus on, he managed to make Mason's evening a little easier. Mason knew he was a lucky man.

Exhausted after such a long day, he pulled off his clothes and collapsed in bed, almost instantly sinking into the hypnagogic state. The desert highway stretched out in front of him, and he jerked awake, thinking he'd fallen asleep at the wheel. It wasn't real, he realized with relief, closing his eyes again.

Later he was far from the desert, somewhere in dense woods, running as fast as he could, dodging the trees. A formless beast was stalking him, and his heart raced with terror. Coming to a river, he ran out onto the bank, but his feet sank deeper into the muck with each step until he was trapped. The massive creature crashed through the brush, not yet visible among the trees, but getting closer. Waking before it appeared, he was relieved to be in the calm darkness of his own room. He forced himself to wake up enough to make notes about it.

Ned was in bed next to him, fast asleep; that was reassuring. He pulled his notepad out of the bedside table and scribbled down what had happened in the dream, then clicked off the light again and snuggled up to his man.

⁂

Ned was gone by the time he woke up in the morning, and Peggy had already left for work. Mason went out to the kitchen and made espresso, gulping the first pot and then savoring the second with his breakfast. Ned had texted him a couple of hours ago, he discovered:

> Meetings on the Westside today.

Once he was lucid enough, he went into the office to make notes for his files about yesterday's events. Writing it longhand on a notepad was time-consuming, and Peggy had once suggested he could get even more old-fashioned if he bought a quill and an ink bottle. But the time it took to write it out helped him think through it, assess things more clearly than if he typed it on a computer. After a satisfying few hours he slid the notes into the folder he'd labeled with Ortiz's name, then added LAURA to the folder's tab.

Effie didn't know anything about séances, and if they were going to do one together, it was going to be Mason's show—he needed to do some reading and figure out how to make it work. He got dressed and swung on his backpack, then coasted down the hill on his bicycle to the boulevard and the metro. Climbing up the stairs out of the station and approaching the central library, he walked past the spot where the military SUV with the bogus plates had been parked. It had only been a couple of days ago, but it felt like ages—so much had happened since.

Not even stopping to check the floor directory—he knew by now where the paranormal books were housed—he headed to the familiar section and found a desk. It was the same one he'd been at when Ortiz's spooks had confronted him, and recalling them gave him a little shiver. He looked around, succumbing to the irrational impulse, making sure there were no suits lurking nearby.

Pulling his laptop out of his backpack, he connected to the library's catalog and started digging. His queries turned up a lot of books about using séances to communicate with the dead. *Learn from Your Ancestors with Easy Three-Step Séances,* offered one, along with *Where Did Granny Hide the Jewelry?: Ask Her in a Safe-Space Séance.* Hanh had once told him that contacting specific people in the spirit world was a Victorian understanding of the technique—for her it was just another way to focus psychic power. A title jumped out at him that might fit with that perspective: *The Séance and the Cosmic Field of Consciousness.* Finding the volume on the shelves, he brought it back to his seat to go through it. The hardback binding cracked like it hadn't been opened for many years. Scanning through it, he found that the author, like Hanh, held that séances were about communicating with cosmic energy:

> The séance is among the most deeply misunderstood psychic tools. Rather than communicating with dead

relatives and movie stars, a true séance provides access to so much more: universal truths that exist independently of time and space.

This is more like it, he thought, and pulled out his pad to make notes.

All the information that exists anywhere is stored holographically, the author explained, in the structure of the universe itself. Anyone could tap into it with a séance, because group-focused psychic energy resonates with the structure to release information. It sounded almost like science, he thought as he scribbled. Explained in these terms, even Ned might buy it.

Eventually he closed the book and sat for a minute, staring at the magazine racks in the distance, lost in thought. He'd only ever done séances before with people who knew a lot more about what they were doing than he did. What he needed was clear instruction on the actual procedures.

Searching the catalog again, he found a likely sounding tome: *Séance Sitting for Dabblers and Dilettantes.* He considered himself more than a dabbler, having participated in a couple of effective group sessions, but all he really needed was an outline. It was an excellent source, he found, once he'd pulled the book from the shelves and returned to his desk to look through it. Rather than presenting canon or rigid rules, the author provided sensible reasoning for why séances were conducted in a specific way, offering some alternatives to the specific procedures.

Making notes on the basics, he came to a chapter

titled "Focal Media." Essentially a focal medium was an object that the séance sitters could focus on, he learned. It wasn't a necessary accoutrement, but for newcomers, especially, it helped with concentration. The focal medium could be a candle flame, a crystal ball or a natural crystal like a geode, or a variety of other objects. One psychic in Florida used a vase of fresh white roses, claiming that staring at the intricate interwoven petals directed the attendees into the right frame of mind. It would be helpful to have a focal medium, Mason decided as he packed up his notes and his laptop—and he knew exactly where to get one.

six

Ned greeted him when he came in, stepping out of the office, still wearing a necktie from his work meetings earlier in the day, the knot loose now and his collar unbuttoned.

"Hey, traveler," he said, embracing Mason. "You were asleep when I got in last night."

"I missed you," Mason said, setting his backpack on the floor.

"Did someone give you a ride from the airport?"

"I actually drove back."

"From Vegas?" Ned said, surprised. "Do tell."

"Will Peggy be home for dinner?"

"That's the plan. Seitan wellington and parsnips."

"So can I tell you about it at dinner, so I don't

have to spin it again for her?"

"Of course. I'm glad you're home in one piece."

"I'm going to chill, but call me if you need help with the seitan."

"Sure," Ned said, and grinned. He never really needed help, especially not from someone with Mason's scant kitchen chops.

Mason stretched out diagonally on the bed, staring at the ceiling, not wanting to sleep, just to decompress. Thinking about trying to inspire Effie with information gleaned in a séance, he knew he had to plan it carefully. She was so capricious and unpredictable—the instructions would have to be clear and straightforward, with plenty of calm opportunity for her to open her mind. He thought about her talking on the phone with Elmer yesterday, speaking in baby talk, and all the pet names she had for him. She was like a ball of energy, expanding in all directions—a whirlwind.

"Hey, shnuggle bunny," Ned said, shaking his arm. "Come and eat."

Mason swam up out of unconsciousness, confused. "What did you just call me?"

Ned chuckled. "I'm calling you for dinner," he said, and left.

When he got out to the main room, Peggy was setting out salad plates for the three of them.

"Hey, stranger," she called to him.

"Were you performing last night?"

"No—I was out with the boyfriend."

"Nice," he said, joining her at the table.

Ned set the wellington on the table, complete with a boat of vegan gravy.

"What a thing of beauty," Mason said appreciatively before they tucked in.

"So how was it working for the hot sailor?" Ned asked, cutting the wellington into slices. "Did you tell him how handsome he is?"

"I didn't, but the other psychic did, repeatedly."

"They hired two of you?" he said, incredulous.

"She's not actually a working psychic," he said. "But Peggy, you were right—it was about an old case. You were both involved in it. Remember Laura?"

"The desert rat?" she asked, her eyes growing wide. "What does she have to do with the Navy?"

He told them about meeting Effie on the plane, about Ortiz, and then finding Laura.

Setting down her fork, Peggy interrupted him. "Wait—they took you to Area 51? Isn't that supposed to be a big secret?"

"It can't be that secret, if we've all heard of it," Ned said.

"I couldn't believe it either when they told us where we were," Mason said. "Its existence might not be secret, but it's definitely a place with secrets. Airplanes were flying around so fast you couldn't even see them. Ortiz claimed there were no flying saucers around, but Laura said otherwise."

"Don't tell Gilbert you were actually there," Ned said. "He'll have an aneurysm."

Mason explained about driving the car back to Los Angeles, omitting the loopier details about the vehicle's paranormal behavior.

"I can't believe Laura showed up in your life again," Peggy said. "She's such a weirdo. Remember out in the desert? She wiped her lips with a napkin, and her lips wiped right off."

"I can't believe you just left her there," Ned said.

Peggy waved her fork. "What was he going to do, take on the whole U.S. military?"

"She told me she could leave any time, but she wanted to do some research," Mason said. "I don't think we have to worry about her. She has collaborators farther up the food chain. That's why they let me leave with her car."

"Nothing would surprise me about that woman," Peggy said.

"Effie sounds like fun," Ned said, pulling his salad plate closer. "My dad would call her a live wire."

"The lieutenant called her a lady. So did her husband, come to think of it."

"Is she European nobility or something?" Ned asked, raising his eyebrows.

"I doubt it," Mason said. "But she seemed to love being called that."

Peggy sang, her voice clear and true: "She's a lady / Whoa, whoa, whoa / She's a lady."

"You should do that song as Peggy Pregnant tomorrow," Ned said, grinning at her. "It'd be hilarious."

"I have done that song. Audiences love it," she said. "And this one's even better." She shifted position, draping her arm over the back of the empty chair beside her, and sang in a deeper pitch, dropping her chin: "Lay lady lay / Lay across my brass bed / Stay lady stay / Stay with me awhile."

Ned and Mason were soon laughing.

"You'd make an excellent lesbian," Mason said. "Very seductive."

"Thanks, darlin'," she said.

"I can't wait to see you busking on Saturday," Ned said. "What time should we come?"

"Whenever. I'll be there from six, and I have to wrap it up at nine."

"What are you going to wear out there?" Ned asked her. "It'll be cold."

"Winter maternity wear," she said, spearing the last bits of lettuce on her salad plate. Meeting his eye, she added, "Seriously. It's a thing."

"That, I have to see," Ned said.

"Too bad you didn't take a selfie with your lady friend from San Pedro," Peggy said to Mason. "I'd love to know how to dress all fancy—you know, like a lady."

He smiled. "I'll try to remember to take one. I'm seeing her again tomorrow night."

"Why?" Peggy asked.

"She has some issues, and needs to get some cosmic guidance. We're doing a séance."

"Just you and her?"

"Plus her husband. Optimally a séance is supposed to have five, but it'll work with three."

Peggy pointed her thumb at Ned. "There are two of us here—that makes five."

"You'd really want to do that?" Mason said. "It

might be a bit dry."

"I'd do it just to meet those two," she said. "They sound hilarious. Ned?" she asked, looking to him.

"It does sound hilarious. I'm in."

"Great," Peggy said. "It's a plan."

"Slow down," Mason said, looking at Ned. "This is my job. You can't sit there and make fun of it, or tell us how delusional we are."

"I don't have to believe it, though, do I?" Ned asked.

"Not at all. But you can't trash-talk it."

"I can behave," Ned said. "I'll do it for the entertainment value."

"And we'll reserve judgment," Peggy added.

"Well, verbally, anyway," Ned said, and grinned.

"You should have them come over here," Peggy said.

"Oh, totally," Ned said, leaning forward. "We can make this table all dark and atmospheric. I'll make snacks."

"Hmm," Mason said, worried now that things were slipping out of his control, that maybe the event was being hijacked. It would be embarrassing if their levity derailed it. But of all the people in the world, these were the two he trusted most. He took a deep breath. "I guess we could do it here. As long as you're taking it seriously."

"Serious as a recession," Ned said, raising his palm. "Hand to god."

"That's completely meaningless from a nontheist," Mason said flatly.

"He'll behave," Peggy said, nodding reassuringly.

"He'd better," Mason said, eyeing Ned.

After he'd helped clean up, he followed Ned to bed. In the dream world, he found himself face-to-face with Ortiz, his blue camo jacket so close that Mason could see the weave of the fabric. "You think that's all there is to it?" Ortiz demanded, leaning too close, his face contorted with rage. "You think that's the end of it?" Mason pulled himself away, struggling into wakefulness, and scrabbled for his bedside pad and pen. He wrote down what he remembered, ending with:

Ortiz extremely angry.

Waking up when his body told him to rather than with an alarm always put Mason in a good mood, and he got up late, pulled on sweatpants and a T-shirt, and stuck his head in the door of the office to mumble a sleepy greeting to Ned, who was well engrossed in his workday. After a couple of navel oranges and bananas and his second pot of coffee, still sitting at the kitchen counter, he called Effie.

"I don't know this number," she answered abruptly.

"It's Mason."

"Oh—hi. What do you need, sweetie? I'm in a bit of a tizzy here. I broke the zipper on my suitcase because it was way too overstuffed. Don't you hate when that happens?"

"Absolutely," he said, even though he had never

had that experience. But it was no stretch to imagine Effie in that predicament. "I won't keep you, but I was wondering if you two wanted to come over here tonight for the séance? My boyfriend and my room-mate will join us, and maybe having five people will bump up the energy level."

"I'd love that," she said, her voice rising. "It'll give us a break from our packing and repacking."

"Great—so we'll see you after dinner?"

"Text me your address," she said, and ended the call.

After he'd sent it to her, he phoned Anna, a colleague in the psychic world. She worked out of a storefront and read palms and tarot cards, a very different approach from Mason's work, but they had collaborated on cases before, and she definitely oper-ated on his wavelength.

"Psychic Center," she answered, the vowels flat-tened in her distinctive Eastern European accent. "How may I direct your call?"

It always made him smile to hear that—she worked in a three-room shop, usually on her own; there was nowhere the call could be directed but to her.

"It's Mason. Do you have some time for me today?"

"Hey, bud—of course I have time for you. Come by after three."

That gave him time to make another pot of espresso, leisurely get dressed, and make his way to the metro. Soon he was carrying his bicycle up the stairs out of the ground in Koreatown, just a few minutes' ride from Anna's shop on Olympic Boulevard.

Riding up on it, even in broad daylight he could see the glow of her neon window sign from a block away: PALM READING and TAROT, and emblazoned on the awning above in large lettering, PSYCHIC.

Locking his bike to a parking sign a few doors down, he opened her front door, the bell above it jingling as he stepped inside.

"Come on through," she called, and he stepped out of the narrow front room, bathed in the orange glow of the window sign, through a curtained doorway into her larger reading room. A round table draped in a black cloth dominated the space, and Anna sat behind it, an array of tarot cards spread out in front of her. With her headscarf and burgundy caftan, crystal jewelry sparkling dramatically in the spotlight aimed at the table from above, she looked the part of the stereotypical storefront seer.

Anna swept the cards into a pile and waved for him to sit. "I just finished up with a client," she explained. "I was double-checking my work."

"That sounds very conscientious," Mason said, flashing her a smile and pulling out a chair, shifting it backward as he sat so that the spotlight wasn't in his eyes. "How's business?"

"*Comme ci, comme ça.*" She gestured expansively. "I'm making the rent. How about you, are you getting jobs?"

"I am—that's actually why I'm here. I'm on a gig, and I wanted to rent something from you. I need a focal medium."

She eyed him dubiously. "You're doing a séance?"

"That's the plan."

"Are you sure? The last time we did that together, things got out of hand."

"It's just a simple session this time. No conjuring—I promise."

"I guess it's none of my business anyway." She sighed and looked away. "What kind of focal medium? You can use anything, you know. A regular old scented candle that costs fifty cents at the thrift store."

"I was thinking I'd use something showy, like a crystal ball."

She nodded. "I have a few of those. Small ones are more powerful."

"Why is that?"

"They focus better. If you want flashy, I have just the thing. How long will you need it?"

"Just a day or two."

She rose and went into the back room, returning a moment later with a little glass ball on a black disk-shaped base. She handed it to Mason. It fit snugly in his palm, but it was heavier than it looked. He rolled it in his hand, seeing the pattern of his palm print adhering to it. It sparkled when he held it in the spotlight, and he saw that the glass had a bluish tint.

"The base has a lamp in it," Anna said. "See?" She demonstrated the switch on the bottom, turning it on and setting the sphere on it. The effect was dramatic, turning it into a luminous blue orb.

"It's perfect," he said. "How much to borrow it for a few days?"

She spread her arms helplessly, as if the question were impossible to answer. "Well, you're a friend, but you're also on a job. Shall we say fifty dollars?"

"Sure," he said, and even though he knew he could probably buy one of his own for that much, he didn't really mind. He was supporting a colleague, and she had sent some lucrative work his way when he'd investigated the man from Grapalia.

"I'll get some bubble wrap," she said, and headed back toward her office. "Payment in advance," she called over her shoulder as she stepped through the curtain.

Mason grinned, pulling his wad of cash from his pants pocket and peeling off the bills. Folding them lengthwise and setting them on the table, he watched as Anna rolled the little globe and then its base into a sheet of bubble wrap. She handed the bundle to him, and he stuffed it into his backpack.

"Let me know how it works," she said, and saw him to the door.

He waved as he went out to the street, the bell tinkling above the door as he left.

Halfway back to the metro, his phone rang, so he stopped in the gutter behind a parked car and pulled it out of his pants. He didn't recognize the number, but it bore a 310 area code. The Westside.

"Braithwaite," he answered.

"Hey, Mason, it's nice to hear your voice."

"Sorry, I can't place yours," he said, pressing the phone to his ear to hear over the street noise. "Can you refresh my memory?"

"It's Iris Yi. We met at a trailhead in the Mojave."

"Of course. How's it going?"

"Do you remember me telling you that I produce television?"

"Sure," he said. He hadn't actually retained that, even though it was only a few days ago.

"I'm working on a show called *America's Filthiest People,* and I'm wondering if you'd appear on an episode and do a psychic reading."

"Seriously? I love that show," he said. "What kind of reading?"

"The episode is about a hoarder, and she needs to find a valuable necklace buried somewhere in the house. It's a pretty intense place—she's a level five."

"Is that bad?"

"There are only six levels, so, yeah, it's very bad. Three feet of trash on the floor."

"I'm sure I could use my psychic insight to locate a piece of jewelry. As long as I don't have to help dig for it," he said. "When and where is the gig?"

"It's a house here in town. Do you have a few minutes tomorrow afternoon? We could meet to talk it over. I'll give you all the details."

"Afternoon works for me," he said.

She gave him the name of a coffeehouse on the Sunset Strip, and he agreed to meet her there at two.

When he got home, Ned came out of the office to greet him.

"There's a possibility I'll be appearing on your

favorite TV series," Mason said. "I got a call from one of the producers today."

"*America's Filthiest People*? That's great," he said. "I guess it was only a matter of time."

Mason laughed, slipping off his backpack. "I'm going to be a psychic consultant, not the filthy person, you ninny."

"That makes more sense. Was it a cold call?"

"I met the woman when I was in Nevada, and I'm seeing her tomorrow to hear all about the job."

"They've never had a psychic on before, but it sounds like a great opportunity for you."

"As long as I don't have to dig through the trash."

"So," Ned said, tapping his watch, "dinner will be earlyish because of our guests. We'll eat when Peggy gets home from work."

"Let me know if I can help," Mason said.

"You're the one who has to make the séance happen, so just focus on that."

Peggy got in soon after, and they ate together at the dining table, green salad and quesadillas made with Ned's vegan gorgonzola. Mason savored each bite, knowing the cheese was a rare treat because it was so time-consuming to make. It took weeks of fermenting the base ingredients in a jar on the counter, followed by more waiting time for the blue mold to grow.

"Can I set up the table for the séance?" Peggy asked.

"That'd be a big help," Mason said, pushing his plate away. "I have some work to do to prepare."

"Are there any decorating requirements or restrictions?" she asked, raising her eyebrows.

"The room should be dark, so we'll need candlelight."

"I was hoping you'd say that."

"I have a black sheet we can use as a tablecloth," Ned said. "It's my understanding that black doesn't dampen psychic vibrations the way gingham does."

Mason considered reminding him that it wasn't a joke, but decided to let it go. They were helping him out by participating, he reminded himself.

"There is one thing that has to be on the table," Mason said, and went to the office to get Anna's mini crystal ball, unwrapping it on the way back and handing it to Peggy.

"It's beautiful," she said, feeling its heft. "Who's going to gaze into it?"

"Hopefully Effie will." He showed her the lamp in the ball's base, then went to the office to look through his notes.

Peggy soon called him back, and he found the living room transformed. They had taken the leaves out of the dining table, so it was much smaller, almost square, and they'd moved an armchair over against the French doors and shifted the table to the center of the floor. Draped in black, the table had the glowing blue ball at the center with several tea-light candles positioned around it.

"I love it," he said emphatically. The three of them stood and surveyed the room.

"Do we need more candles?" Ned asked. "I only

put out a couple, but we could go bigger."

"Let's see," Mason said, and stepped to the wall to click off the room light. "It looks good to me," he said, and turned it back on.

"Now that that's settled," Peggy said, "What do I wear? I've never been to a séance before."

"Doesn't the mall by your office have a séance-wear shop?" Ned asked. "You should have dropped in there."

Ignoring him, Mason shrugged. "Wear whatever you want. It's not a formal thing."

"That's easy for you to say," Ned said. "You'll be wearing the burgundy caftan and the headscarf."

"It's so weird that you said that—the woman I borrowed the crystal ball from was wearing exactly that outfit."

"Don't get any ideas," Ned said, holding up his palms. "I'm not psychic. It was an easy guess—it's what they all wear."

"Something dark, maybe?" Peggy said.

"I'm wearing what I have on, so don't steal my look," Mason said.

"Summer plaid in the middle of winter? No one is going to steal that, not ever. You have to wear something else. Nedly, what look are you going to be working?"

"I'm thinking aloof but taciturn skeptic," he said.

"What does that look like?" Mason asked dubiously.

"A black turtleneck and dark-rimmed glasses."

"You don't wear glasses."

"I do for séances."

"You two are no help," Peggy said, and went down the hall.

"You'd better hustle if you're going to get dressed," Mason said to Ned. "They'll be here soon."

"Let's do it," Ned said, and Mason followed him to the bedroom.

"Do I really need to change?" Mason asked.

"In the spirit of the event, why not? Clothes make the man, and it's your party. What image do you want to project?"

"Like I know what I'm doing."

"We can make that happen," Ned said confidently, and opened Mason's side of the closet, flicking through the hangers. "How about the gray-green shirt with the olive necktie?" he said finally, pulling them out.

"They're both kind of green. Don't they clash?"

Ned held the shirt and tie together against his chest. "The olive pops out against the shirt, see? It's fine."

Mason peeled off his shirt and put on the one Ned had chosen, then tied the necktie. Looking at himself in the floor mirror, he realized it really did look good.

"Can we put some product in your hair?" Ned asked.

"That sounds like a dangerous precedent. Why would we want to do that?"

"You'll look sleeker." He went into the bathroom and returned with a little jar of pomade, and spent a minute reaching up, slicking it into Mason's hair, carefully adjusting it. Finally he was satisfied, and stepped back. "See? Now you look like you know what you're doing."

Mason checked the mirror, turning his head to see the sides. "You really do have a knack for this."

"It's my birthright as a gay man," Ned said simply.

"So why didn't I get that gene?" Mason muttered, and went out to the living room.

Peggy was wearing a plain mustard-colored blouse with cap sleeves.

"That's a cute top," he said.

She did a double-take when she saw him. "Looking good, Mason," she said happily.

"Don't sound so surprised," he said.

"Ned picked it all out, though, didn't he?"

"A-yup."

Ned joined them, as promised wearing a black turtleneck, heavy black-rimmed glasses, and black jeans.

"You look like a beatnik," Mason said, looking him over.

"Thank you," Ned said. "I'll take that as a compliment."

Ned went to check on his canapés, and soon the doorbell rang.

"Showtime," Peggy said, and Mason went to the door.

seven

Elmer and Effie hadn't dressed up for the séance—she was wearing a sweater and jeans, with the red plastic button earrings, and Elmer had on chinos and a dress shirt that struggled to stay tucked into his pants. Mason greeted them as they stepped in, and introduced everyone. Effie handed him a bottle of wine.

"I love the tie," she said, reaching for his neck and delicately smoothing the knot. "Very 1950s."

"1952, actually," Mason said, involuntarily lifting his chin at the uncomfortable proximity. "It's vintage."

"Can I take your jackets?" Ned asked.

"Mason didn't tell me you were Latino," Effie said, slipping off her coat. "When I heard your name,

I thought you'd be Anglo."

Ned leaned toward her and spoke quietly, as if sharing a confidence. "It's actually Edgar," he said, pronouncing it with the clipped Spanish vowels, "but somehow it got shortened in a very Anglo way."

"I love it," Effie said, touching his arm. "That's so LA. Don't you love this big crazy city? So much diversity."

"I do, and I'm glad you see the value in that. Not everyone does." He went down the hall with the coats, and Effie turned to Mason.

"Such a nice place," she said. "I love the table—so moody."

"Let's relax a minute before we get into that," Mason said, holding up the wine bottle and moving toward the kitchen.

He heard Peggy ask them to sit as he dug for the corkscrew in a drawer, then poured four wineglasses. Ned came in and pulled his plate of canapés out of the oven with a kitchen towel. He poured Ned a tonic water, and they took everything out to the coffee table. Peggy was in an easy chair, and Elmer and Effie were sitting close together on the sofa, Effie's hand in Elmer's lap. Ned sat with them, and Mason took the other chair.

"These are so elegant," Effie said, delicately picking a canapé off the plate.

They really were, Mason thought—a swirl of pesto pocked with almond slivers on little squares of crispy bread.

"Ooh, and they're warm," Effie said. "Heaven."

"You showoff," Peggy said, eyeing Ned and taking a canapé, examining it critically before biting into it.

"It's not a contest," Ned said. "Some people's canapés are just more elegant than others."

"To new friends," Effie said, raising her glass.

They toasted with her, and Elmer turned to Ned after he'd taken a sip, glancing at the black turtleneck.

"Are you a psychic too?" he asked.

"Oh, god, no," Ned said, absently pushing up his glasses. "I work on mortgages for real estate brokers."

"Oh, yeah." Elmer nodded. "Real estate is fun."

"Sometimes," Ned agreed. "It's hard to guess right about market movement. What do you do?"

"I'm an entrepreneur. I'm thinking about my next project right now." He took a sip of wine and quickly turned to Peggy. "What about you, young lady, are you a psychic?"

She smiled. "Mason's the only one in the family. I work with lawyers."

"Really?" Elmer said, a flash of concern in his eyes. "In the DA's office?"

"In a private practice. My firm does a lot of Wall Street work."

Elmer looked relieved. "I hate lawyers. Except the good ones. When you get one of those, they're invaluable."

"Nah," Peggy said. "I kind of hate them all."

Elmer laughed, and tipped his wineglass toward her.

"Mason said you work in a hotel," Ned said, looking to Effie.

"It's the Casabunda in Long Beach. We get mostly business travelers."

"I've heard of it," Ned said. "It's upscale, as I recall?"

Effie nodded, sipping her wine. "Super fancy. I have to wear a uniform. Corporate types expect a lot from the help, but when you problem-solve for them, they can be grateful."

Ned frowned. "In what way?"

"They tip well. Not always—there are some cheapskates—but if I hustle, I usually get paid."

"Nothing wrong with getting paid," Ned said, reaching for a canapé.

"Do you two have kids?" Peggy asked.

"We're not on that plane," Effie said. "Our lives are far too evolved. Having children … it's like scrabbling around in the mud. We're soaring high above it." She raised her hand toward the French doors, wiggling her fingers, following them with her gaze, longing in her eyes.

"Maybe they're like lawyers," Peggy said. "You just have to get the right one."

"Our advanced level of sexuality precludes a life with children," Elmer said gravely.

"Wait," Mason said, frowning. "I thought sex was how you *got* children."

Ned snorted, setting his tumbler on the coffee table.

"In case you can't tell, he's kidding," Peggy said.

"Mason said you were going on a cruise," Ned said. "That sounds like fun."

124

"It was my shnuggle bunny's idea, to renew our wedding vows," Effie said, leaning toward Elmer and nuzzling his neck.

"Like on TV," Ned said.

Effie looked back at him, her brow furrowed. "I guess.... Can you believe my wedding dress still fits? I'm taking it to wear on the ship when we have the ceremony."

It should fit, if you only got married two years ago, Mason thought, taking another canapé. "I was there when Elmer broke the news," he said. "You were pretty excited."

"Of course I was. It meant that I'm going on an adventure with my prince." She turned to Elmer, kissing him on the mouth. He closed his eyes and lingered, getting deeper into it, both of their mouths working.

Mason cringed, and Ned shook with silent laughter, more at Mason's expression than at the behavior of their guests.

"So you and Mason met on your road trip?" Peggy asked, raising her voice.

"That's right," Effie said, pulling away from Elmer and absently fluffing her hair. "I didn't want to do it, drive all that way when there are perfectly good airplanes, but I agreed because of my little psychic issue." She glanced toward the black-clad table, concern in her eyes. "Which, hopefully, we'll address tonight." Turning back to Peggy, her tone was lighter. "It wasn't so bad, although I would have loved to stop in Vegas and work the slots, maybe shoot some craps.

Mason raced through on the freeway at ninety miles an hour, hunched over the wheel like a maniac. I got whiplash trying to get a glimpse of the bright lights. It went by in a blur."

"Wait a minute," Mason said, sitting up in his chair. "You were complaining about how slowly I was driving. And we agreed not to stop."

Effie turned to Peggy. "Funny how a man can lay down the law, and that means, 'we agreed.'" She waggled her fingers in air quotes.

"I know how that goes, sister," Peggy said, reaching over to clink her wineglass on Effie's.

"You make me sound like a bully," Mason said sharply, feeling the color rise to his face. "I'm not."

Effie looked to Ned, her brow furrowed. "Is there always this much drama with this one?"

Ned laughed. "Well, I guess I'd have to say that dramatic events have been known to happen around here."

Effie cackled and slapped her thigh. "Mason, you're a hot mess."

"Are you kidding me?" Mason demanded, glaring at Ned, but he was looking at Peggy, exchanging a knowing glance. He could feel his face burning. "I am not a drama queen," he said, trying to keep his voice even.

"Of course not, sweetie," Peggy said. "But sometimes your work tends toward the dramatic."

"Oh, my god," Mason exploded, but swallowed his retort, willing himself to calm down. He folded his arms and looked at Elmer. "She desperately wanted to get back to you, you know. In the car she couldn't talk about anything else."

"That's my gal," Elmer said, grinning and wrapping an arm around her.

Mason scowled at Ned. "'Dramatic events have been known to happen.' It sounds like when a corporation issues an apology. They don't say, 'Sorry we killed eight thousand people.' They say, 'Mistakes were made.'"

"It's called diplomacy, sweets," Ned said, mirthful behind his glasses. "And you can't honestly say your life is free of dramatic events."

Mason sighed. "I guess that's true."

"So let's get rolling on the séance, shall we?" Ned said. "This is nice, but I don't really want to watch you all get loaded."

Mason slurped the last of his wine, getting up and moving to the table, then stood with his hands on the back of the chair closest to the French doors. It seemed like the one that would provide the least distraction from the city lights outside.

"Does it matter where we sit?" Peggy asked.

"Anywhere is fine," he said, and pulled out his own chair, mentally shifting gears to focus on the work ahead. Peggy sat beside him, and Effie came around to his other side, with Elmer beside her and Ned between him and Peggy.

Once they were all seated, Mason cleared his throat. "I'm grateful that you're all willing to be here to help me try to help Effie. The purpose of this séance is to open channels for information from beyond the physical world." He looked at each of them in turn, and noticed that Ned was listening, bright-eyed behind his fake glasses, no hint of skepticism in his expression. In that moment he was grateful for him too, his earlier irritation melting away.

"Some séances are about conjuring spirits, or talking to individuals," he continued. "This one is intended to channel insight and inspiration for Effie. Ideally, by the end of it, Effie will know what to do about her issue."

"So what do we have to do?" Elmer asked.

"It's traditional that we all put our palms flat on the table," Mason said, demonstrating briefly with his hands firmly on the black tablecloth, fingers splayed. "We'll relax for a minute and clear our minds, and I'll verbalize the question we want answered. Effie can do that too," he said, looking at her. "Talk about what you need to know. Articulate it however you want."

"OK," she said, concern in her eyes.

"We'll all concentrate on the question, with only that in our minds. You can close your eyes if you want, or focus on the crystal ball. You might see something in the ball, or you may feel something; or there might be nothing. In any case, try to generate energy for Effie to harness and use."

Elmer nodded, and Peggy grinned at Effie encouragingly.

"I forgot the lights," Ned said, and leapt up to switch them off.

The room fell into darkness, only their faces

visible in the flickering candlelight. When Ned sat down again, his black shirt made him look like a disembodied head floating above the table. The blue glow of the crystal ball was evident now, a soft focal point at the center of the group.

"Spooky," Effie muttered.

"Let's put our palms on the table, and clear our minds," Mason said, trying to speak slowly and calmly. "Focus on the ball, or the candle flame, or the empty space in your mind. Don't think about your day. Tune out the mental chatter about what you have to do tomorrow. No thoughts, just emptiness. Breathe slowly, deeply."

Ned's gaze was fixed on the blue ball, a little grin on his face. Elmer's eyes were uncomfortably screwed shut. Mason closed his eyes and calmed his own mind. He tried to sense the energy in the room, but couldn't decide if he was detecting the vibe of the group or if it was just something he wanted to be there, but maybe wasn't. He pushed his extrasensory awareness outward, visualizing it as expanding to encompass the five of them.

"We're here to get insight into Effie's issue," he said finally. "What can she do to fix it? How can we help her fix it?"

Effie spoke, loudly, as if addressing someone in the next room. "Help me out, oh, wisdom of the universe," she said. "I blew it. Splintered all over the place. Give me a chance to fix things."

They sat in silence, hands on the table. Mason looked absently at the crystal ball, not really seeing it but focusing on any potential insights that might drift into his awareness.

There was something moving, he realized, not inside the ball but on the surface, in the tight curvature of the glass. A reflection, he thought. But no, the room was dark, and nothing was moving; it wasn't that. Images flitted across, bouncing, dancing in the blue. It was the camouflage pattern Ortiz wore, he saw with a start, drifting across the surface like clouds in the sky. And Johnson, the suit at the library, her hair tightly pulled back, her face distorted by the curvature, but still identifiable.

Anna had been right—the little ball seemed like a powerful tool, but so far nothing germane had appeared, just things that had already happened, the echoes of memories.

Bam! The table shook with a sudden blow. Effie let out a little shriek, and Peggy and Ned jerked their hands off the table.

"Jesus H. *Key*-rist," Elmer said.

Mason felt a surge of adrenaline welling up. He'd been lost in the images on the crystal ball, not paying attention to their collective energy.

"Who kicked the table?" Ned demanded.

"Nobody kicked it," Effie insisted, her tone shrill. "It's a message from beyond."

"Not a very articulate one," Ned said.

"What do we do?" Peggy asked, looking at Mason. "It feels like the spell has been broken."

He looked at Effie. "Are you feeling any inspiration?"

130

"That scared me," she said, still agitated. "Does that count?"

"Let's try again," Mason said. "Palms on the table, clear our minds, focus our energy on Effie." Closing his eyes, he tried to sink back into the calm and empty state of mind, but his heart was pounding. He could hear Elmer breathing heavily, almost panting.

After a minute Effie let out a sharp sigh. "I can't do this, Mason. I'm too freaked out."

Mason opened his eyes and took his hands off the table. "I get it. Could you get the lights?"

Ned got up and switched on the room lights, causing everyone to wince in the sudden glare. Mason blew out the candles.

"I'm sorry," Effie said, absently arranging her hair. "It just wasn't happening."

"Take some deep breaths," Peggy said.

She did, and nodded appreciatively, then spoke more calmly. "It felt menacing, like a dragon was standing right outside, and we were trying to wrench open the door."

"Interesting," Ned said. Mason glanced at him; he was being sincere, watching Effie closely.

"It was worth a try," Mason said to her.

"Just my luck," she said. "Snake eyes."

"Wait—you saw a snake?" Mason asked, confused.

"It's just an expression," Elmer said. "In craps, snake eyes is a low roll. It means you lose."

"So it's a Vegas thing?" Mason asked.

"It means this isn't a solution for my lady," he

said, exasperated at Mason's obtuseness. "The splinter thing has been completely stressing her out, and here we are, tits up on the pavement."

An image flashed through Mason's mind: Effie and Elmer sprawled on their backs in the parking lot at their apartment building, shirtless, groggy, gazing at the sky.

"Maybe, maybe not," Mason said. "Sometimes psychic work takes time to percolate. We'll give it a day or two. Some insight might appear."

"Maybe when we're on the cruise," Effie said hopefully.

"I'm not holding my breath," Elmer said. "Listen, thanks for your hospitality, but we've got an early morning."

Ned rose. "It was lovely to meet you both."

Effie hugged all three of them in turn and made her way to the door. Waiting for Ned to fetch their coats, she said to Peggy, "Let's get lunch sometime, sweetheart."

"I'd like that," Peggy said.

"Call me when you get back from Cabo," Mason said as they left.

"Well," Ned said, closing the door behind them, "as the man said, here we are, tits up on the pavement yet again."

"You are not allowed to start using that expression," Peggy said, sinking into one of the easy chairs.

Mason chuckled, joining her on the sofa, and picked up a canapé, popping the whole thing into his mouth.

"So am I correct in thinking it didn't work?" Peggy asked him.

"I don't think it did. Effie didn't get any useful information."

"I didn't feel anything," Ned said, joining him on the sofa, "except that knock on the table. Please tell me you kicked the leg."

"I certainly didn't," Peggy said.

"I had nothing to do with it either," Mason said. "None of us would have done that. It's a physical side effect of the concentrated psychic energy. It's probably all about Effie, but I don't know what it meant. I was getting other information from the crystal ball."

Ned frowned, pulling off his fake glasses, but didn't respond.

Peggy looked thoughtful. "I'm not sure if I felt anything psychic, but it was pretty intense. That might be regular old pheromones, not psychic energy."

"At least you got something out of it," Ned said to her. "You and Effie have a lunch date."

She grinned. "I might just do it. She's pretty entertaining."

Mason realized he was tired, the intensity of the evening wearing off. "Thank you both for indulging me."

"Totally worth it. Now I know how séances work," Ned said.

"It was fun," Peggy said. "But I think I'm going to bed. Can you two handle the cleanup?"

Mason picked up the wineglasses and ate the last

canapé, and Ned folded up the black tablecloth. They pulled on either end of the table to put the leaves back in, then shifted it back to its usual place.

Once he'd put Anna's crystal ball in his desk and toweled the pomade out of his hair, Mason peeled off his clothes and climbed into bed, turning to face Ned, who was reading on his tablet.

"I'm so glad you were able to be part of that without debunking it," he said, rubbing Ned's belly.

Ned set his tablet aside and moved closer. "I'm not a zealot. Plus it helped me understand a little more about your career. You were so confident and authoritative, telling us all how to do it."

"It was mostly bluster, but yeah, I know what I'm doing."

"I like that. Maybe you should tell me what to do," Ned said, running a hand over Mason's chest.

Mason grinned and pulled him closer. He was worn out, but not too tired for sex.

Afterward they spooned for a while, and Mason quickly drifted into sleep. On a dark street he found himself confronted by Effie, standing in front of him, glowering. They were in New Orleans, he knew that much, but he didn't know how he knew. There were no visual clues, just a quiet city street. Effie was dressed like the suits in the library, and put her hands on her hips, pushing back the folds of her jacket to reveal a shiny gold badge clipped to her belt.

"I'm not the bad guy here," she snapped.

"I never said you were," Mason said, holding up his palms and stepping back.

He knew it was a dream, knew he could manipulate it if he could become just a little more aware, then maybe tease some insight out of it. But the environment drifted away from him, and eventually he managed to wake up, clicking on the light and wincing as he dug for his pen and pad, hastily scribbling what he remembered:

> Effie in New Orleans
> had a badge
> "I'm not the bad guy"

It seemed to take a long time to wake up, hauling himself up out of the depths, forcing his eyes open. Maybe all the psychic energy he had invested in that massive waste of time last night had drained him, pushed him deeper into unconsciousness. He'd told Effie that something still might come out of it, but that was just spin. It had been a failure, and he knew it, could feel it. Thinking about that as he lay in bed, gazing at the daylight beyond the window, blinking to stay awake, it felt pretty depressing.

Ned wasn't around, and Friday was a workday for Peggy, so the house was quiet. He took his phone out to the kitchen but didn't have the energy even to glance at it until he'd had some coffee, fumbling with the espresso maker and eventually managing to fill the little pot, then sat at the counter and sipped at it, slowly catching up to this reality.

There had to be other ways to sort out Effie's thing,

he knew, but he needed to do more research before he got there. Maybe that had been part of why the séance had been a bust: he didn't have a firm handle on what Effie had actually done. The library wouldn't be useful until he knew what he needed to look for, so he planned to spend the day on web research.

In the office, he pulled open his laptop and sat at his desk, searching for references to energy avatars. A lot had been written, much of it relating to hauntings, but nowhere could he find any mention of a projection gone awry. There was a fairly well-researched article about how to ramp up the power of an intentional projection, something the author called "psychic shouting," and even a whole book about unintentional appearances of energy avatars and how to curb them. After several hours of digging, he was getting frustrated—none of the sources shed any light on Effie's incident.

His phone rang, a welcome interruption, and he folded his computer closed before pulling it out of his pants. The caller ID said it was Pretty Nail Blowout.

"Thanks for bringing my car back," Hanh said when he picked up.

"I'm sure there's quite a story there," Mason said. "Do you have some time today? I wanted to talk to you about some other stuff."

"Do your nails need work?"

Mason examined them. "I suppose I could use a buff."

"Swing by later today. I have 3:30 open."

He got up and went out to the kitchen, grinning

to himself. Things were working out. He'd have plenty of time for his meeting with Iris before that, and Hanh would definitely have some insight about Effie.

There was leftover pesto from Ned's snacks in the fridge, so he toasted some sourdough bread and spread the slices with a thick layer, munching on the last of it as he walked down to the bedroom. Getting dressed for the cold and slinging on his backpack, he left in plenty of time, pulling his bike out of the garage and cycling all the way, down to the boulevard and then the few miles to the Strip.

After he locked up his bike in the parking lot, he went inside and bought an espresso at the counter. The place was bustling but he found a table, and positioned himself so he had a view of the door. He could have seen her with his eyes closed, he thought, when Iris appeared in the doorway, dressed like a schizophrenic again, in four different shades of red and orange and pink. She saw him right away and joined him, setting her black folio bag on the end of the table.

"You look good," he said. "Can I get you a coffee?"

"I can never eat or drink when I'm talking about the show," she said with a rueful smile.

"Because of the subject matter?"

"Precisely. Filth and food don't mix."

"I'm glad you called," he said. "Although I was surprised that you did. I thought maybe my companion was a little rude when we met."

"She might have been, but I don't really remember that," she said. "What was her name again?"

"Effie."

"Are you close?"

"I just met her. A friend asked me to give her a ride and help her talk through some stuff."

"That's very gallant of you."

"So what's the job, exactly?" he asked, sipping his espresso.

Iris shifted in her chair. "The woman in this episode has lost her grandmother's precious necklace in the hoard. You'd be on camera for a short time trying to help her locate it."

"Does it matter if I can find it or not?"

"Not at all," Iris said, raising her eyebrows. "It's reality TV, so whatever happens, happens."

"No pressure on me, then," he said, and smiled. "Can I ask why you're using a psychic? I watch, and it doesn't fit the pattern of the show."

She nodded. "We're changing things up a bit this season, revamping the stylistic elements and giving the regular characters some more depth."

"The shrinks and the cleaners," Mason said.

"Right."

"The one problem I foresee is that I'm not exactly photogenic."

"The pretty people are on scripted series," she said. "Reality TV is about real people, not good-looking ones."

"Gee, thanks," Mason said, frowning. Being photogenic wasn't the same as being good-looking, but clearly she didn't think he was either one.

Iris met his eye, oblivious that he felt affronted.

"None of our people are models. You'll do fine."

Mason nodded. "What's the pay like?"

"It's a full day's work, early morning until late afternoon, and we retain all the rights to your image from that day. For that we pay twenty-five hundred."

"That's good money for a day's work," Mason said, raising his eyebrows. "It makes it an attractive proposition. I'll consider it carefully."

"We're filming the episode on Monday," she said. "I'll need an answer today."

"Wow—that's soon."

"It might help you grow your brand, if that helps you decide," she said. "One of the cleaners has built a serious business based on the series. People from all over the country hire her to declutter their houses."

"That kind of money is definitely enough to compensate for the embarrassment I'll face," he said. "Count me in."

"Good," she said, clearly pleased. She opened her folio and pulled out a sheet, handing it to him.

Scanning it, he saw that it was a list of the support staff who'd be working that day, the work hours, and the address.

"Usually an episode has one cleaner and one shrink, right?" Mason said. "Which ones are doing this episode?"

"Ray and Dr. Connie."

"I like Ray," Mason said, grinning. "The other cleaner is mellower, but Ray gets emotionally involved, so it's more fun. Which one is Dr. Connie, again?"

"She always wears hoop earrings and a low-cut blouse."

"Oh, right. She isn't the most empathetic of the shrinks, but I like her. She seems smart."

"I'm glad you approve of my staff," Iris said, raising her eyebrows.

"It's nothing personal," Mason said. "It's just television."

"Just television is how I make my living," she said intently. "You think it's like junk food you buy at a gas station, rather than a gourmet meal? A coloring book for dunderheads rather than a weighty Russian realist novel?"

"I guess I find the show entertaining more than inspirational," Mason said slowly, hoping he wasn't causing further offense.

"What's that thing people say? 'All feedback is good feedback.' In the industry nobody ever really trashes anyone else. It's considered gauche. So I guess I'm not used to it. But I know that kind of attack stuff is all over the internet."

"I didn't mean it as an attack," he said, frowning.

"Don't worry about it," she said, folding her folio closed, clearly ready to leave.

"So what time should I show up at this place?" he said, avoiding her gaze and looking at the sheet she'd given him. The location it listed was a street address in Lawndale, which he knew was way south; it would take him ages to get there.

"We'll send a car for you. Work starts thirty minutes after sunrise, so it'll be early. Call the transportation number there," she said, pointing it out on the page, "and tell them your address."

"Sweet," Mason said. That simplified things immensely.

She stood and gave him a little air kiss before she left, pushing aside her earlier consternation. Watching her go, a flurry of warm color, he marveled at her sensitivity. Most actors and industry people he knew had learned to develop a thicker skin.

Finishing his espresso, he went out to the parking lot to retrieve his bike. Hanh's shop was a short ride away, straight down Sunset. Glancing at the clock on his phone, he saw that he'd be right on time.

Walking into the salon, he was greeted by the same receptionist he'd met when he dropped off the car on Tuesday night.

"The red man," she said cheerfully. "Welcome— nice to see you again."

He could feel his face heat up. Maybe that's why she called him that; more than just the red hair, he was always flushed with frustration when he came here.

"The name is Mason," he said pointedly. "I have an appointment with Hanh."

"Go ahead," she said, gesturing into the shop.

Hanh came out of the back and directed him to a nail station. She seemed lighter today, despite her severe wedge haircut, greeting him with a smile. He sat across the little table from her, and she set to work on his hands.

"With all the paranormal stuff you do, I'm amazed you have time for this," he said.

"Doing nails is relaxing," she said. "Plus it connects me to the community."

"The last time I saw you, I caught a glimpse of your wings." It had been an unusual encounter, far from home, right after he and Peggy's boyfriend, Matt, had been trying to decide whether Hanh was a garuda. So much of it fit—garudas were winged, and they policed paranormal activity, which seemed to be one of Hanh's roles.

She smirked, still focused on his nails. "That's absurd. You were in an altered state, imagining things."

"I don't believe that for a second," he said, but he knew better than to press it any further. "Why did Laura have your car? I know it's not really a car, by the way."

"Of course it's a car—among other things. She was working."

"Why did she get pinched for smuggling cobalt 60?"

"Is that what they told you?" she said, pausing her work and looking up. "She wasn't doing that. There are lots of other sources of gamma rays." She went back to work, deftly trimming Mason's nails. "Of course the military would think it's something dangerous. Threats are their job, so it's all they see. It was just a mishap, and we could have undone it, but we decided to work with it."

"For research purposes."

"Very astute," she said, grinning to herself. "I'm glad you could help with the car."

"It was a long ride home with Effie."

She had to pause her handiwork to laugh. "My understanding is that you'll get paid for your time."

"Absolutely, and I'm not complaining," he said. "Do you know anything about Effie and her energy projection incident?"

She eyed him and gestured for him to switch hands. "That's why you're here. It's a mess, and we need to fix it."

"Laura said it was like an interference in the field, something like that."

"Imagine a crowded train station," Hanh said, focused on his hand. "Everyone is walking in all directions, maneuvering around each other when necessary. It looks chaotic but it's really highly organized, and it all works. Everyone gets where they're going in the minimum amount of time. But then a tanker car of maple syrup spills, and it floods the station, a couple of inches deep. It's only a little syrup, and no one is going to drown, but everyone has to wade through it, and it slows everything down, and pisses everyone off. That's what Effie created."

"That does sound problematic."

"I don't know how she did it. She's not the greenhorn she claims to be, but she's also not aware of what she's capable of. And I know," she said, glancing up at him, "that she can't fix it on her own, despite Laura's plan to approach it that way."

"It's interesting that you're not both on the same page."

"We are, eventually. She's a pedagogue, and figures

we should let people learn from their mistakes, fix their own messes. I'm a little more pragmatic: 'Let's just fix it.' But I'm not opposed to her methods."

"I get it," Mason said. "So what can we do about Effie?"

Hanh grinned, dusting off his nails and releasing his hand. "Laura already asked you that."

He nodded. "I tried one route already. We did a séance to tap into the universal knowledge base. I thought Effie might get inspired and come to a solution herself. But it didn't work—the table shook, and Effie got rattled. I'm thinking now that your assessment is accurate: she can't fix it on her own. We're no farther ahead after the séance than we were when we started."

"OK," Hanh asked, eyeing him. "So what's next? If she can't fix it alone, how do you suppose we can undo the damage?"

"Is this a test? I'm sure you have solutions mapped out that I couldn't even imagine."

"Even so, what would you do?"

"It might be kind of simple-minded, because it's based on stuff I already know how to do," he said, briefly glancing at his nails. "The séance didn't work, so I'm not confident this will either." He sighed. "I thought I might use the bleed-through technique. I'd go back before she did it, and tell her not to do it."

Hanh nodded. "Remember when we bled through at the racetrack to stop that nickel-and-dimer, Ali?"

"Of course."

"Remember how uncooperative he was?"

"Completely uncooperative. You had to shove him."

"Why would Effie be any more open-minded, considering she wouldn't even know you?"

"Good point," he admitted.

"Do we even know exactly when it happened?"

"Laura and I looked in on the event, but I don't know when it was. Can't you tell?"

"I could estimate," Hanh said, "but it would be easier to ask her. Is she feeling any remorse?"

"It seems like it, yeah."

"Let's use that to our advantage. Why don't you have a talk with her, and figure out when we could approach her to prevent her little fracture?"

"So you like my plan," he said, grinning. "I love that you think it's a worthwhile idea. I thought it might not be."

"We'll see how it plays out." She rose from her seat. "How are your nails?"

Mason stood up and examined them, frowning in mock concentration. "Not bad."

Hanh laughed. "That's the best manicure you've ever had, and you know it."

After he'd paid for the work at the front desk, he retrieved his wheels and started off for home. The pedals felt lighter after talking with Hanh. It was exhilarating that she and Laura were consulting him on problem-solving, including him in the process. It made the failed séance seem like a detail now, already fading in significance. And it wasn't like he was being press-ganged into it either, which Matt had been worried about; no, this felt like a cozy inclusion, a warm swimming pool with shallow steps leading down into it, not a leap off the pier into the pounding winter Pacific surf.

They'd also given him the option several times not to be involved, and they even made sure he was getting paid. If he'd reacted differently, he realized, he could have walked away from it, not even noticing the opportunity they had designed for him, laid out for him, made his for the taking. But he hadn't walked away, he'd seized it, taken in seriously. He pedaled harder, grinning to himself. He loved this—it felt like real progress.

Before dinner he worked at his desk, labeling a new folder EFFIE BROWNSTEIN and writing up notes about Laura's request, the séance, and his meeting with Hanh. Ned came into the office well after darkness had fallen.

"Hungry?" he asked, wiping his hands on his kitchen apron.

"I guess I am, yeah," Mason said, looking up. "Whatever you're doing smells great."

"It's kind of a tomato-and-rice thing. We'll name it if we decide we like it."

"Where's Peggy?" he asked, following Ned out to the table, which was set for two.

"Rehearsing, I suspect. She'll be back later."

They ate, and it was delicious, of course, and Ned tasked him with coming up with a suitable name for his concoction, spiced with thyme and made with tomatoes he'd canned last summer.

"Do you want to watch an episode of *Pica Confessions*?" Ned asked as they cleaned up. "I saw the preview. This woman eats wax crayons. She says each color tastes different. Her teeth look like a pride flag."

"How fun is that?" Mason said, and they watched the nausea-inducing episode together, gasping at each fresh horror.

Climbing into bed, he felt content and sated, and thought that might translate into some productive time in his dreams. But all he saw in the netherworld were jumbled shapes and colors, a seething mess. It seemed so meaningless that he didn't even bother to wake up and write it down.

eight

When he got up, Ned was sprawled on the sofa with a book, enjoying his quiet Saturday morning. Mason made himself a pot of coffee, then another, and once he felt awake enough, joined Ned, sitting on the other end of the sofa.

"Do you remember the name of the hotel where Effie said she worked?" he asked.

Ned set his book in his lap. "The Casabunda, in Long Beach."

Mason nodded, typing it into his phone. A search brought up an image of the lobby, decorated in black and purple and ornate shiny metallic wallpaper.

"Have you been there?"

"No, but someone I work with had meetings in

their conference rooms. He said it's upscale, but not one-percenter upscale."

"Got it," Mason said, tapping at his phone to save the hotel's address. "Your parents went on a cruise once, didn't they?"

"Years ago, but yeah, they did."

"Do you remember if they were able to use their cell phones on the boat?"

"I think they try to make the environment on those cruises as much like home as possible," Ned said. "So I'm sure your phone would work. Are you thinking of calling Effie on her trip?"

"I'm not sure if I should. I don't really want to interrupt her do-over wedding, even though they've only been married for two years."

"Two years? Seriously?" Ned said, his eyes growing wide. "I guess that explains all the cuddling and the lip-lock. They're still in the honeymoon phase."

"Is it just that, though? I don't know many couples who are so glued to each other. We certainly aren't."

"We could be," Ned said, grinning at him. "Shnuggle bunny."

"Oh, hell, no—do not be calling me that."

He laughed. "I guess it takes all kinds. I think you should call her on the ship. If she doesn't want to talk to you, she won't pick up."

"You're right," Mason said, rising. "That's completely logical—thanks."

Opening the French doors, he took his phone outside. It was cold, and the balcony would be in shadow for hours yet, but he wasn't planning to be out here long. He leaned on the railing, looking out over their hilly little neighborhood, and dialed Effie's number.

"Who's this?" a man's voice answered, gruff and abrupt.

"I thought I was calling Effie's phone," Mason said.

"This is Effie's phone. Who's this?" He spoke in an African American dialect, nothing like Elmer's.

"My name is Mason. I'm an acquaintance of hers. Who are you? Are you on the boat with them?"

"Harbor Police. When's the last time you saw Ms. Brownstein?"

Mason hesitated. "Uh … I'm not sure I should be talking to you."

"Man, just answer the question. I've got your phone number, and your name is here on the caller ID. If you make me track you down, I promise, you will regret it."

"Why would you come after me?" Mason said. "I'm just some guy on the phone."

"I don't know yet. But I'll definitely pop you for interfering with my investigation."

"Jesus, man, relax. I saw her on Thursday evening. What are you investigating?"

"Where did you see her that day?"

"At my house," Mason said. He was passing the point of extricating himself, he could feel it. The image of a spotlight came to mind, twisting slowly around to shine on him. He closed his eyes and visualized the beam continuing away from him, pushing it along with his mind.

"Do you know Elmer Brownstein?"

Mason sighed. "He was here that night too. What's going on?"

"Effie's at Beth Israel Hospital in Long Beach."

"I thought they were on a cruise. What happened to her?"

"That's what I'm trying to find out. You're one of the last people to see them together. You and I need to talk. My name is Detective Kerr. Can you come to the port today?"

"I can't believe this," Mason said. "I want to see her. I'm going to the hospital. I'll come to see you after that."

"She won't have much to say. She's in a coma."

"What?" Mason sputtered.

"Does that surprise you?"

"I have to go," he said, hanging up without waiting for a reply. Sinking onto the cold patio chair, he sat for a minute, thinking it through. She'd been fine two nights ago, full of energy. What on earth had happened to her?

It was too cold out here to concentrate. Rising and pulling open the French doors, he went inside, strode past Ned, went into the office, and opened his computer. He needed to talk to Elmer. A web search for his name turned up only a couple of possible matches. One implied that Elmer worked in insurance, but Mason couldn't find a phone number for him, not even the name of a company. He sat back in his chair. If Elmer was with her at the hospital, he could talk to him there, ask him what happened. But it was possible that Elmer was also hospitalized. He should have asked the cop about that.

Striding back into the living room, he said to Ned, "Effie's in the hospital. I'm going to Long Beach to see her."

His eyes grew wide. "What happened?"

"I don't know yet. A cop answered her phone and wouldn't give me any details. Maybe I can find Elmer."

"I'd offer to drive you," he said, "but—"

"No," Mason interrupted, shaking his head. "I can handle it. It's not like it's in Siberia."

"Be careful," Ned called after him as he went down to the bedroom to get dressed. "Let me know what's going on."

It was pointless to be impatient with the trip, he told himself as he rode down the hill, pedaling to gain speed and streaking around the curves. No matter how fast he rode, it was going to be a long schlep to Long Beach.

Two trains and over an hour later, he was locking up his bicycle in the rack at the hospital. In the lobby he found the front desk and asked for Effie. The receptionist typed the name into her computer and studied the screen.

"She's in the ICU. No visitors. Immediate family only."

"I'm her brother," Mason said. "Is Elmer with her? If I can't go up, maybe you could ask him to come down and talk to me."

She gave Mason the once-over and checked her screen again. "Do you have an ID?"

He handed it over and watched as she swiped it through a reader, then handed it back with a visitor pass.

"Wear it high on your shirt," she instructed. "Ninth floor, left off the elevators. Tell the nurses why you're there."

"Thanks," he said appreciatively, clipping on the pass and walking toward the elevator lobby.

The nurse's station in the ICU was an island in an open floor that was ringed by beds housed in glass-walled cubicles. Some were vacant, but several had patients in them. Every one of the little rooms was crammed with electronic equipment.

"I'm here to see Effie Brownstein," he told a woman in maroon scrubs who was sitting at the station's desk. A glance at her ID revealed her name to be Vega.

She looked him over and fixed her gaze on the visitor's pass for a moment before she spoke. "The police have been sniffing around for her," she said, with an accent that he guessed might be Tagalog.

"That's nothing to do with me. I'm a relative."

"You know she's unconscious, don't you?"

"I'd like to see her anyway," Mason said.

Vega sighed. "I'll take you to her unit."

"Is her husband around?"

"No," she said flatly, rising from her chair, and led him to a room with the curtain pulled across it, obscuring its occupant. She paused at the doorway, turning to Mason, then stepped closer to him, looking up at him and glaring. "No drama," she said through clenched teeth, poking him hard in the shoulder, twice, to accent each word.

Startled, he took a step back, intimidated even though she was a full head shorter than him.

"What is it that you think I might do?"

Ignoring his question, Vega pulled the curtain aside, exposing the clear wall and the doorway, and stepped in.

Vega's odd assault was forgotten the moment he saw inside. Effie looked like she was sleeping peacefully, albeit with tubes in her arm, wires sprouting from inside her hospital gown, and flickering machines all around. Thankfully she wasn't intubated. A wave of sadness swept over him, a lump forming in his throat. He hadn't expected that. He didn't know her very well, but it was jarring to see anyone incapacitated that way.

It was surprising that she still had her blond curly hair. It must be her own, he realized, not a wig. The nurses wouldn't have left it on. Vega gestured for him to enter and pointed to the lone chair. He stepped in beside her and sat down. After looking him over suspiciously and glancing at Effie, Vega left them alone, resuming her watchful post a few yards away.

Perched on the edge of the chair, he stared at Effie. In the absence of Elmer, he wasn't sure now what point there was in coming here. It struck him that she was psychic too—maybe he could connect with her mind. He considered taking hold of her hand, but no, that was too much, and might incur the wrath of Vega. He closed his eyes and spent a minute calming his thoughts, focusing on expanding his mind. Projecting the words toward her, he thought, *Are you in there? What happened to you?*

He waited, trying to sharpen his focus, to get deeper into a receptive state of mind, but there was no response, not even a glimmer.

Vega's voice drifted into his awareness: "He's praying for her." He opened his eyes and saw her just outside the glass, standing with a bald guy in a plaid suit who towered over her.

"I'm not praying," he said.

Vega scowled and waved for him to come out. Her companion was as tall as Mason, dark-skinned and thick-bodied, with meaty hands, sunglasses hanging from his breast pocket. Only a guy with real swagger could pull off such a loud color combination, tan with red running through it; on Mason it would just look silly. His identity was evident from the shiny badge clipped to his belt.

"Detective Kerr," Mason said.

"Very good," Kerr said. "Maybe you really are psychic."

"You checked into my work?" Mason asked, straightening his back, trying to make himself as tall as the cop.

"What are you talking about?"

"You know that I work as a psychic."

He snorted. "A cursory internet search told me that much."

"This is an ICU, not a country club," Vega said, raising her voice and waving her arm.

"Isn't it funny," Mason said, eyeing her, "how the people who complain about drama wind up generating most of it?"

Her face hardened. "Get out, both of you."

"This way," Kerr said, chuckling to himself, and led Mason down the corridor.

"What is her damage?" Mason asked. "She's so rude."

Kerr just snorted and stepped into a waiting room, comfortably carpeted and ringed with chairs and magazine tables, but currently devoid of people. He went over to the TV set, blaring with an update about an exciting new product, and silenced it.

Turning back to Mason, Kerr looked him over, hands on his hips. "I bet you hate airplanes as much as I do."

Mason stared at him, confused. "Airplanes?"

"You're tall, like me. Airplanes aren't very comfortable."

"That's true. It's like sitting on kindergarten furniture."

"Do me," Kerr said, grinning at him.

"What?"

"Do a psychic reading. I'm not going to pay you, but what do you pick up? You know, 'I'm sensing the letter M ... Mother ... Michael ... Minnesota ...'"

"I'm not that kind of psychic."

"Well, what can you do?"

Mason sighed. "Show me your ring. I hate being

tested, but I might be able to read it."

It was a simple gold wedding band, and Kerr pulled it off, struggling momentarily to get it over his knuckle, then handed it to him. Mason closed his eyes and cupped his hands over the object, feeling its warmth.

"What do you see?" Kerr asked.

"Give me a minute." It didn't take long to get into the empty-mind state, as he'd just been doing it at Effie's bedside. He waited for some insight or inspiration, and gradually an image coalesced. A sea of colorful boxes—shipping containers, he saw— methodically arranged. Not on a ship, though; they were stacked in just a few layers, spaced well apart on the ground. His perspective swooped down into one of the boxes, through the steel top. It was dark inside, and hot, and humid, but he could see what was here: black plastic bundles, sealed with packing tape, and the skunky smell of weed.

Mason opened his eyes. "You made a big drug bust at the port. I saw a shipping container full of pot."

"How about that," Kerr said, raising his eye-brows. He reached for his ring and slid it back on his finger. "Of course, that could be a calculated guess, knowing what my job is. You could have read about it in the newspaper too—it was a while ago, but it was part of the biggest drug bust on the West Coast in years."

Mason could feel his cheeks burning. "See, that reaction, right there, is why I hate being tested. Didn't I say I hate being tested?"

"All right, settle down," Kerr said, moving his hands to his hips again, revealing his badge, gleaming hypnotically, in itself an admonition to behave. He studied Mason's face. "What were the Brownsteins doing at your house two days ago? Were you working for them?"

"It wasn't for work. They dropped by for drinks. Strictly a social call." No way was he going to mention the séance, and get mired in a whole explanation of that.

"How long have you known them?" He pulled out a little notepad and flipped it open, jotting in it as they talked.

"I just met Effie this week—Tuesday. I gave her a ride home from Nevada. We were in the car together for hours, and when I dropped her off, she invited me in to meet Elmer. So I was at their apartment briefly that evening."

"What was the vibe between them when you went to their apartment, and at your place?"

"They were fine. When I drove her home, she'd only been away for a day, but they acted like it had been weeks. They were very passionate—kissing, pawing each other. Happy."

"No arguing, no disagreements? Maybe after a couple of drinks?"

"Nothing like that. They had some wine, but they don't really seem like drinkers."

"In the car that day you must have had plenty of time to chat. Was there any talk of problems between them?"

"None at all. She just talked about how much she missed him."

Kerr nodded. "What time did you leave their apartment on Tuesday?"

He thought for a minute. "It was just before eight. I remember because I was trying to get to a shop in Hollywood that was closing at nine."

"And Thursday? What time did they leave your place?"

"Not late—before eleven. They were both sober. I don't know who drove."

He made a final scribble and flipped his notepad closed. "Well, yesterday they boarded *The Pearl of Primordial Chaos* for a five-day Baja cruise—"

"That's the name of a ship?"

Kerr shrugged. "Some Chinese cruise line. Anyway, Effie took a swan dive off the balcony of their stateroom. She fell forty feet into the drink."

"That's awful." Mason shook his head in disbelief. "How far out to sea were they?"

"The ship was still in port. She went in between the boat and the dock, so it was easy to fish her out, at least."

"It must have been an accident," Mason said. "She wouldn't have jumped. She was perfectly happy the night before. They were going to renew their wedding vows on the boat."

"Like on TV," Kerr offered.

"That's what I thought too."

"Witnesses put Elmer right there with her on the balcony. One witness said maybe he tried to grab her to save her from falling. Another thought maybe he pushed her. Any ideas?" he asked, watching Mason closely.

"They seemed so into each other. I can't imagine he would do that—but I don't really know them."

"Key witnesses said there was an argument in progress."

Mason shook his head. "It's so weird. Where's Elmer? Have you asked him what happened?"

"We have him in custody, but he's not saying much."

"So you think he did it."

"I'm more interested in what you think."

"I have no idea," Mason said emphatically. "What's Effie's prognosis?"

Kerr shrugged. "The docs say there's no serious damage. She's unconscious from the trauma, but she should recover." He waggled his notepad, looking thoughtful. "You said you met her in Nevada. What were you doing out there, exactly?"

"Right," Mason said, nodding and scrambling mentally to come up with a version of the story that didn't include all the paranormal elements.

In the doorway he saw a familiar flash of maroon: Nurse Vega.

"Detective," she said excitedly, catching his eye, "She's awake."

Without a word Kerr followed her toward the ICU. Mason followed, just a few steps behind them, thankful for the interruption.

As Kerr approached Effie's room, now bustling

with activity, Vega stopped him and went inside. Kerr and Mason stood at the glass, watching a nurse in green scrubs working with the electronics, and another woman in a white jacket, presumably a doctor, Mason thought, talking to Effie, who was now propped up in the bed. Mason watched Kerr for a minute, staring through the glass, his gaze intent. He was straining to hear what was being said. Effie was speaking to the doctor, but her voice was inaudible from here, and she seemed weak.

Eventually the doctor gestured for Kerr to come in and stepped away from the bed. Mason moved to follow him, but Vega stopped him at the doorway.

"You'll have to wait, Red. Too many people in here."

Kerr was conversing quietly with the doctor in the small space, but Effie had spotted Mason outside.

"Mason, is that you?"

He waved through the glass and flashed her a smile.

"Come in here, sweetheart. It's such a relief to see a friendly face."

Vega didn't protest, stepping aside to let him enter.

"I'll do the talking," Kerr said pointedly, catching Mason's eye.

Effie waggled her fingers at Mason, so he stepped around to the other side of the bed and took her hand.

"It's so good of you to come and see me," she said, her voice weak, her expression a little dazed.

"I'm glad you're awake."

The doctor left, and Kerr sat down in the lone chair, shifting it closer to the bed and leaning toward Effie.

"My name is Detective Kerr. Harbor Police. Do you remember what happened on the ship?"

"Where's Elmer?" she asked, her eyebrows furrowing.

"We've got him in lockup," Kerr said calmly. "He can't hurt you now. Did he push you?"

Her expression hardened. "I have no memory of what happened."

"I think you do," Kerr said. "You don't have to protect him. He won't get to you—I'll make sure he can't. But to do that, you have to tell me what happened."

"There's nothing to tell," she said flatly. "I have no memory."

Kerr sighed, sitting back in his chair. "In that case, I'm going to have to let Elmer go. He'll be able to come over here and visit you. Is that what you want?"

Effie turned to the nurse in green. "Don't let him in," she said, her voice rising. "I never want to see him again."

"So he did push you," Kerr said.

"I didn't say that," she snapped. Then, more calmly, "Listen, officer, I'm tired. Can you leave me alone?"

Vega spoke up. "Time to go, detective."

Kerr rose, reluctantly, and pulled out his business

card, pressing it into Effie's palm, then clasping her hand in his big meat hooks.

"If you change your mind, call me any time, night or day," he said, and then stepped out.

"You too, stretch," the nurse in green said, looking up from the computer screen she was working on. "Vamoose."

"I need to talk to her."

"Out," Vega said, raising her voice and glaring at him.

"No—Mason, stay with me," Effie pleaded.

Vega sighed. "Five minutes," she said, and left.

"At least sit in the chair," the other nurse said, annoyed.

Mason stepped around the end of the bed. Effie reached for his hand again when he sat down.

"It was terrifying, seeing the water come up at me like that," she said. "I thought I was done for. I tried to turn it into a dive—you know, like at the swimming pool. I don't actually remember hitting the water."

"Too bad you hadn't seen it coming. Your déjà-vu thing."

"I did see it coming," she said, her eyes growing wide. "I didn't know how it would happen, or when, and then it just happened."

The nurse stepped out of the room, leaving them alone for a moment.

"Did he push you?" Mason asked quietly.

She pulled her hand away, agitated. "Don't ask me that," she pleaded.

"OK, calm down," Mason said, glancing toward the nurse's station. "I spoke to my colleague about your psychic projection issue."

"Oh, that," she said, as if it was something long forgotten.

"When, exactly, did you go up to Ojai?"

"It was Sunday afternoon, after my shift. I didn't want to be home because of the stupid football program Elmer always wants to watch."

"This past Sunday?"

Effie nodded. "Why all the questions?"

"It'll help us figure it out," he said. "You saw it coming, right? Laura called it an energy avatar, but what was the word you used for the experience?"

She thought about it. "It felt like shifting all my energy outside my body into that place, into the trees."

"Before it happened, what did it feel like was going to happen?"

"I guess I anticipated that it would be like splintering into multiple parts. Like splitting an apple into wedges, or the segments of an orange."

"What time did you get there?"

"I worked eight to two, then drove up there, which takes less than two hours, so it was probably around four, and I spent an hour or so. It was getting dark, so I drove home."

"You worked eight to two," he said, repeating it to store it in his memory. "You worked until two at the Casabunda."

"That's the place. It's the best hotel west of St. Louis."

"Of course," he said, nodding, even though that sounded like a spurious distinction. "You were on the front desk on Sunday?"

"The concierge desk. It was a slow morning. Most of our guests are Monday-to-Friday business travelers, so weekends are usually quiet."

"And that's in the lobby?"

Before she could answer, the white-jacketed doctor stepped in.

"Sir, you'll have to go now," she said. "We have work to do here."

He rose, squeezing Effie's hand. "I'll see you soon."

She smiled wanly as he left. Clearly she didn't want to be here, but at least she was conscious.

Riding down in the elevator, he took some deep breaths, shaking off the intensity and chaos of the hospital ward. It was a relief that she was lucid—it meant he could move forward with his plan.

nine

On the long metro ride back to his part of town, he texted Ned:

Effie out of coma and on the mend. I'm home for dinner.

A reply buzzed in his pocket a moment later:

Great news. I'm out running errands. See you at home.

It seemed quixotic to try to write notes while he was standing in a swaying train car with his wheels, but he decided to do it anyway, positioning his bicycle so it wouldn't fall over or roll away, and then swinging his backpack around and pulling out his yellow pad. He had to pause and catch his balance whenever the train stopped suddenly, but mostly it worked, and he spent the trip writing about Effie's fall, Detective Kerr, and what Effie had said about Elmer. He drew a double box around the last line:

jumped, fell, or pushed?

A few minutes before reaching his stop, he phoned Pretty Nail Blowout. Listening to the ring, he wondered why Hanh didn't have a cell phone. If she really was a supernatural being, perhaps she couldn't actually use one.

"Pretty Nail Blowout," the receptionist answered in her familiar high-pitched singsong.

"Is Hanh in today?" he asked.

"Yes, but she's with a client."

"Will she be there for the next hour or so? I want to drop by."

"She's working all day. Please visit our salon."

Soon he was climbing the long stairs out of the ground, bicycle under one arm, and then rode the few blocks to Pretty Nail Blowout.

"Welcome, Mr. Mason," the receptionist greeted him when he pulled open the door.

"Thanks," he said appreciatively, deciding not to point out that Mason wasn't his surname. It was a huge improvement over "red man."

"Ms. Hanh is in the office. Go on back."

He found her stacking little white towels on the wire racks in the back room.

"You really do work here," he said.

"Of course I do. It's my business, Mason." She

grinned at him, puzzled. "Help yourself to coffee."

Mason turned over a mug and poured a cup from the battered old coffeemaker by the sink, then joined her at the worktable, pulling out a chair and setting his cup down as he sat.

"How did it go with Effie?"

"She filled me in on the timing. She said it happened Sunday afternoon. Before that, she worked until two at a hotel in Long Beach."

"So what's your solution?" she asked, raising her eyebrows.

He sipped carefully at the acrid liquid before replying. "We should go to the hotel that day and tell her not to do it."

"You think preventive action is preferable to addressing the issue reactively?"

"I can't answer that, because I'm completely clueless about what could be done now. I don't have a lot of tools, but the bleed-through is one that I know, and I think it might work."

She nodded. "And you believe we should go to her workplace rather than visiting her home?"

"I thought about that," he said. "When I was with her in Nevada, she was quite taken by the military people. Awed by them, actually, and one man in particular. The most effective approach might be to pose as authority figures and tell her she can't do it. I think she'll listen."

A grin spread across Hanh's face. "An elegant solution," she said. "Of course it would have to be all about men." She thought for a minute. "Let's ask your friend Matt. Two strapping males will be more effective than me and you."

"Good idea. She doesn't know him."

"Last Sunday, she didn't know you yet either, correct?"

"You're right," he said, and grinned. "Things get confusing when they happen out of sequence."

"Can you talk to Matt, and find out if he's free tonight, or maybe tomorrow night? We'll go late."

"So the three of us will go talk to her?"

"Just you two," she said. "You should work out exactly what to say to her. I'll come along to help with the bleed-through, but you'll be making contact."

"I'm seeing Matt this evening, so I'll let you know. Do you have a cell phone?"

"Just leave word at the front desk, or on the machine."

"If Matt can do it tonight, what time?"

"We'll meet here in the alley at eleven."

"Cool," he said, and nodded. "What's you're receptionist's name?"

She grinned. "It's Tran."

He walked out through the salon, and flashed the receptionist a smile before he pushed open the door.

"Thanks, Tran," he said, and she smiled at the acknowledgment.

Cycling home, he realized Hanh was letting him take the lead, by having him reason out the approach they were taking and then implement it. Usually he just followed her instructions, not always sure exactly what was happening. He had to grin. Despite the fear that his plan might not work any better than the séance, it was gratifying to be trusted.

Ned and Peggy were out when he got home, the house quiet. After he unwound and ate some leftovers, he sat on the sofa and called Matt.

"Are you up for some psychic work tonight?" he asked.

"I already have plans. Peggy's busking in NoHo. Aren't you going?"

"Yeah, I am—this is later."

"Oh … damn it," Matt said. "Hanh?"

"Exactly. We're taking a short trip to Long Beach."

"How far back?"

"Less than a week."

"Well, I guess that's a relief. At least it's not a fucking decade."

"There's a bit of prep work involved," Mason said, and outlined the job.

"Maybe I can come home with you after Peggy's thing, and we can work at your pad?"

"Perfect. And bring a change of clothes—think business-casual plainclothes cop."

After he'd ended the call, he left word at Pretty Nail Blowout for Hanh that they were on for tonight, then went into the office and grabbed his laptop. Back on the sofa, he searched the news to see if there had been any reporting about Effie's fall. He immediately found an article from a South Bay newspaper.

> Long Beach—A San Pedro woman remains hospital-ized after a four-story plunge into the harbor from a stateroom balcony aboard *The Pearl of Primordial Chaos*. The incident happened while the cruise ship was still moored at the pier. Effie Brownstein, 52, and her hus-band, Elmer Brownstein, 56, had boarded the ship less than an hour earlier for a trip down the Baja Peninsula.

It was a shock that Effie was only fifty-two; she could easily be in her sixties. The article went on to say that Elmer was being questioned about the incident, but provided no theory about what had happened, only that "the investigation is continu-ing." Scrolling down, he found a photo. Elmer and Effie were standing almost cheek to cheek, beaming and looking into the camera, Effie in a blue striped sailor top and green button earrings, Elmer in a loud orange Hawaiian shirt with sunset silhouettes of palm trees. They stood behind a decorative life ring, mostly cropped out of the image for the newspaper but with part of the ship's name still legible on it: PRIMORDIAL.

Copying the article link, he emailed it to Ned and Peggy, adding a note: "News item about Effie. Scroll down for the image."

Eventually Ned got home, and Mason came out of the office to greet him.

"I want to hear about your day," Ned said, after they'd kissed, "but maybe in the car? I'm going to make burritos now because it's quick."

"That definitely takes precedence in my book," Mason said.

They sat at the counter to eat, Ned changed into a dark shirt, and they both took jackets for the cold evening. Ned pulled the Barracuda out of the garage, and on the drive to the Valley, Mason told him about his trip to the hospital, and Effie, and Kerr.

"Are you going to try to figure out what happened?" Ned asked. "How she wound up in the drink?"

"Nobody asked me to, and the cops are already doing that, so no—I'm out of it."

"Good," he said emphatically. "Dude sounds unbalanced, if he threw his wife off a boat. He was fine when they were here, but you never know what's going on with people."

"It might have been an accident."

"Still—you don't need to mess with that."

"I'm glad we're going to see Peggy early," Mason said, changing the subject. "Hanh has some work for Matt and me to do later tonight."

"She seems to do a lot of psychic stuff on the side," Ned said, dubious. "Running a salon must leave her a lot of free time."

"I don't think time really matters to her."

"What time is your 'work'?" he asked, lifting a hand off the steering wheel to put air quotes around the word.

"Late," Mason said, ignoring the skepticism. "But Matt and I are going to do some prep beforehand."

"That works for me. If you're leaving with him, I'll go to a meeting in Hollywood. Tons of people come out on Saturday night. It's the hardest night of the week to stay sober."

Ned found a parking space on the street not far away, and they walked the few blocks to the pedestrian mall, which was just a regular shopping street that had been blocked to vehicular traffic, an extreme rarity in LA. They soon found Peggy, positioned on the pavement not far from the shops, already strumming and singing a cheery folk song. They joined the handful of other people watching her and found Matt, who greeted them wordlessly, not wanting to detract from the music, waving without taking his hand out of his duffle coat. He wore several days' stubble and his brown hair was unkempt, but he was smiling broadly as he watched her play.

Peggy nodded to acknowledge them. She was dressed for a long evening in the cold: a wooly cap dotted with fabric daisies, a heavy jacket in a psychedelic paisley print draped over her massive fake belly, and bell-bottom jeans. Her boots were hard to see but Mason could tell they had sizeable platform heels. He tuned in to the lyrics.

> I've never been one to chase after you, baby
> Living in the moment, living on your love
> But I don't even need to look for you lately
> 'Cause here you are, the one that I'm dreaming of.

A couple of other pedestrians stopped to join the onlookers as the song progressed, and when she finished, many of them clapped, and a few threw coins and folded bills into her open guitar case.

"Thank you," she said, massaging her belly and

wincing slightly, which elicited a few more cash contributions.

She launched into another song. It was fun to watch her, and to see how other people were enjoying the music. After the song Ned wandered off and came back with a tray from the coffee place, hot cider for the four of them. Peggy finished her subsequent number and took a break, wrapping her fingers around the paper cup for warmth.

"I love this," she told them. "People are digging my music."

"It's great that you're playing your own stuff," Ned said. "It has way more power because it's your own words, your own feelings."

"We're going to leave during the next set," Matt told her, and took her empty cup. He kissed her good-bye, patting her enormous belly under the paisley jacket. Peggy picked up her guitar again, and as she started into a tune, another spectator, holding an infant, caught Matt's eye.

"So you're the father?" she asked, smiling at him.

"Oh, hell, no," Matt said. "That's nothing to do with me. I'm just her boyfriend."

Ned snorted, suppressing a laugh, and the woman stepped away, a confused look on her face.

After clapping at the end of the song, the three of them made their way toward the cars. Mason kissed Ned good-bye when they got to the Barracuda, and Matt led him farther down the block to his SUV.

Driving back through the hills, Mason explained his plan.

"So we both have to be authoritative?" Matt asked. "Or is it good cop, bad cop? I think I'd have to be the bad cop."

"I ran across two goons from the military this week. They had to use a secondary tactic on me to get me to talk to them, but I know what they tried to pull on me at first actually worked on Effie. Let's use that as a starting point," he said, and related the encounter in the library.

"We'll need to make fake military IDs," Matt said, braking with the sea of taillights in the slowing freeway traffic.

"Isn't it a felony even to think about doing something like that? Maybe we should say we're from some other organization."

They talked about it, hammering out the details, and soon pulled up on Mason's street.

"Peggy has a bunch of design software, so we'll use her computer," Matt said, locking his car and walking with Mason toward the house.

"Do you know her password?"

"Of course, man. We've been dating for ages."

Mason frowned, unlocking the front door and pushing it open. "I don't think Ned would know how to get into my computer, and vice versa."

"Don't you trust him?"

"It's not that…. I guess it just never came up. I don't know if he would even care." Thinking about it, fleetingly, he'd bet money that Effie knew exactly how to get into Elmer's computer.

In the living room they spent some time talking

about what they were going to say, anticipating Effie's responses, tweaking the banter. They did a run-through, and then another, until they were both satisfied.

"I need to make the ID. Bring me your driver's license so I can copy the picture," Matt said, and went down the hall into Peggy's room. Mason followed him in, looking around in wonder at the disheveled bed, the piles of paper, the clothes strewn around.

"Wow. I rarely come in here. The girl room is a lot more hectic than the boy room."

"That's because Ned is so well organized," Matt offered, sitting down at her computer.

"Or maybe because Peggy has more clothes than the two of us put together."

"More than all three of us, I suspect." He started some software on the computer, then took Mason's license and examined it. "You look like you just won a stuffed toy at the fair in this picture. We want to look tough."

"Maybe you could take a new picture?" Mason said, and then remembered his passport. "Give me a second." He went into the office and found it in his desk, then brought it back to Matt, who was already working on a layout.

"This is perfect," Matt said, grinning at the photo. "You look disappointed as fuck, like the merry-go-round just broke down."

"The photographer told me I wasn't supposed to smile."

"Do I use your real name?"

"No—for this kind of thing, it's Mason Ruth-erford."

Matt chuckled. "OK, then," he said, and turned back to the computer.

Mason went to his bedroom to pick out clothes, eventually settling on a dress shirt and black pants, like the Navy guy who'd confronted him in the library had been wearing. He was standing there in his underpants and socks when Matt came in.

"What?" Mason demanded, turning around to face him, embarrassed, feeling the color in his cheeks. He considered covering his crotch with his hands, but that would just make it worse.

"Do you have a wallet that looks all officious?" he asked, oblivious to Mason's nakedness or his discomfort. "We can't very well flash a flimsy piece of printer paper. It needs a cover."

"I'm sure I do," he said. "I'll bring it to you."

Matt left, and after Mason had pulled on his pants and fastened his belt, he went into the office and dug around in the desk. He found an old bus pass holder, from back in the day before everything went to electronic cards. It was black, the most officious color of all, and had a plastic window to display a card. He took it in to Matt and went back to finish getting dressed, then went into the office, digging through Ned's desk drawers to find his old pair of mirrored sunglasses, which he tucked into his shirt pocket. Waiting for Matt, he went to the kitchen to graze. That burrito had been hours ago.

"It's fucking perfect," Matt called to him.

Going into Peggy's room to examine the fake ID, he had to smile. "It *is* perfect."

"I used an image of a military ID as a template, then your sad-as-fuck passport photo. You're a natural, Mr. Rutherford."

"Don't you need one too?"

"You said only one of the Navy people showed you an ID, right? I think it should just be a small part of it, not some formal dual procedure. It keeps us in charge."

"That actually makes sense. I'll be the one with the ID."

"You don't want to hand it to her, either, just flash it."

"Right," Mason said. "That's what the Navy woman did with me." He practiced folding it open with one hand and holding it up for Matt.

"Too fucking long," Matt said. "I could read everything. Show it for about half that long."

Mason flashed it again, then folded it closed and shoved into his pants pocket.

"That was good—just enough time to see your photo and read a line or two." He glanced at his watch. "Are we ready?"

"You have to change."

"I forgot," Matt said, his eyes growing wide. "I have the square clothes in my car." He sprang up and ran out, the front door slamming a moment later.

By the time Mason walked out to the living room, Matt was back, with a pair of gray trousers and a dark-blue shirt on a hanger. He tossed a pair of black oxfords on the floor with a clunk, and then unbuttoned his pants and dropped them right there, kicking them off into a heap and pulling on the dressier pair. Mason had to smile. He envied the guy's complete lack of self-consciousness.

"Do I look like a goon?" he asked, once he was fully dressed, spreading his arms.

"Almost," Mason said, pointing to his head. "Except the hair."

"Seriously?" Matt said, running his fingers through it. "I kind of let it go when I'm not in the classroom."

"We want the whole operation to be flawless."

Matt sighed. "That's true."

"Ned has some hair stuff. You'll look like a goon in no time."

Matt followed him into the bathroom and scooped a gob of the waxy pomade onto his fingers, then rubbed his hands together and ran it into his mane. After a minute's effort with a comb, he looked dramatically different. Older, Mason thought.

"This is actually really good stuff," Matt said, admiring his handiwork in the mirror. "It doesn't feel oily at all."

"For all I know, you just put six hundred dollars' worth of product on your head," Mason said, standing in the doorway. "Ned does not mess around with his grooming products."

Matt laughed and turned his head, checking out the sides. "Good enough?"

"You really should shave too."

"I was afraid you'd say that," he said.

"You can use my razor."

"Gross. What if I catch mange—or worse?"

"You can use a new blade. It's perfectly hygienic." Mason pulled it out and installed a fresh blade, handed it to him, then went out into the hall. He stopped, and turned back, standing in the doorway. "I don't have mange," he said pointedly.

Finally they were ready, the pair of them looking sharp and serious.

"Are you going to be warm enough?" Matt asked as they left the house. "They said it might drop into the forties tonight."

"I'll be fine," Mason said, locking the door behind them. "We're going to daytime, remember?"

Climbing into Matt's car, Mason was on edge, apprehensive about the job. Matt was in the same place, he could feel it.

"We're really well rehearsed," Mason said, looking over at him as he navigated down the hill.

"Damn right," Matt said, keeping his eyes on the road. "And we look like a million bucks."

"So how's it going with Peggy?"

Matt grinned. "Good, I think. Stable. She makes me happy."

"Right on."

"Since you took her to meet that guy with the spinning machine in his yard, though, she's been interested in electronics. I'm worried that it'll become an obsession. She already bought a soldering iron, which at this moment is sitting on my kitchen table."

"It probably won't last long," Mason said. "She goes through phases—there have been way worse ones. When she was learning cuneiform writing, she needed the equivalent of wet clay, so the house was full of plaster of paris for weeks—in the sink, in the bathtub. I was glad when that one ended. Vegan fruit tarts were a bad one for me too. I was gaining weight."

Matt laughed. "I guess she has a short attention span."

"Not at all. She learns enough, and perfects it, and then moves on to the next field of interest. She's a renaissance woman."

ten

Matt parked on a side street near Hanh's salon, and the pair of them walked into the alley. She was already waiting for them in her beat-up little car, parked at the back door to Pretty Nail Blowout with the lights off, her silhouette just visible in the shadows. Mason waved at her as they walked up.

"You two look great," Hanh said, rolling down the passenger-side window and leaning toward them. "Like cops who are trying to dress like they're not cops."

"That sounds just about right," Mason said.

"I could drive," Matt offered. "My vehicle has more room."

"It has to be this car," she said. "Get in."

Mason pulled open the door and folded the seat ahead, climbing into the backseat.

"I drove this thing back from Vegas," Mason said, once Matt had buckled himself into the passenger seat. "It's not really a car. Do you need it for the bleed-through?"

"Of course it's a car," Hanh muttered, pulling out of the alley and onto the boulevard.

"What's not carlike about it?" Matt asked, turning to look at him.

"Well, I drove it five hundred miles and never put any gas in it. When I left Vegas it had Nevada plates, and by the time I got to LA it had Cali plates."

"Huh," Matt said. "Like James Bond's car?"

"I don't think it's a mechanical thing. The plate became something different."

Matt turned to Hanh. "If it's not a car, what the hell is it?"

She was focused on negotiating the traffic on the freeway ramp, but spoke once she had merged across a couple of lanes.

"It *is* a car—look at it. But you're partly right, there's more. Its existence is connected to several instances of itself at once, so that it can share information."

"That doesn't sound different, or paranormal," Matt said. "I'm connected to several instances of myself at once—I'm the person I was yesterday, and I share information with myself by remembering what happened."

"Is it more like Laura's thing, where there are multiple copies of her floating around?" Mason asked, leaning ahead between their seats.

"It shares information with itself in both directions, not just as memory," she said.

"But it's not what it looks like," Matt said. "The car form is like a disguise, or a cloak?"

"It's not subterfuge. Nothing in this world is merely what it looks like on the surface—you know that. Everything has layers, and components, and history. What's unique about this car is that it's built from a lot of ideas, while most cars, most things, are a single instance of an idea."

"You've lost me," Mason said.

"When you hear the word *rock,* you know what it means," Hanh said, her eyes on the road ahead, "and there are millions of variations—so many sizes, colors, and shapes. But in your mind you have an image of it. When you see one in the external world, you think *rock.* It's a single instance of that idea. This car is more like the idea you have in your head. It's not a single instance but an aggregate of what a lot of people assume a car looks like. The only thing about it that's subterfuge is that being an aggregate, most people won't give it a second glance."

"Wow," Mason said. Looking out at the freeway and the oncoming cars flashing past, he tried to absorb her explanation.

"I guess I get it," Matt said. "But why is it thirty years old? Most cars aren't."

"So that it's not an anachronism any time nearby.

It doesn't have to change anything to shift twenty years. If it went to where it was fifty years ago, then it would look different. But shifting that far involves other complexities."

Neither one of them spoke as the ideas seeped in. Hanh focused on the freeway, driving fast in the light traffic.

"Some car," Matt said finally.

Hanh chuckled. "So are you two ready?"

"We have a plan," Mason said.

"Good. Let's hope it works."

In the rearview mirror, lit by the oncoming traffic, he could see she was grinning faintly.

"So if we convince this woman not to splinter," Mason said, "then Laura won't have to summon her to Nevada, and I'll never meet her. Doesn't that kind of break causality?"

"Nevada will happen anyway," she said. "It's a persistent event, regardless of what changes today."

"But when I meet her in Nevada, she'll remember me from tonight."

"She won't remember. It's a separate event."

Matt turned toward her, confused. "Does that happen in a parallel stream, or is there only one? How does that all work?"

"How do you think it works?"

"How the hell should I know?" he said, throwing up his hands. "I have trouble enough navigating my own life. Like coming to terms with the fact that I'm not actually riding in a car right now."

Hanh laughed at his outburst, but didn't say

anything. Matt watched her for a minute, hoping for something more, then sighed and looked out the window.

Exiting the freeway, Hanh navigated the surface streets to a parking structure with a sign over the entrance that read HOTEL CASABUNDA. She drove up several levels and parked far from the walkway to the hotel, against an outside wall, where there were few other vehicles. They climbed out and Mason stretched, glad to be able to arch his back after riding in the confined space. He saw now that Hanh was dressed up: a dark skirt and a white blouse with a blue sweater, three strands of pearls around her collar. She was even wearing makeup, which made him realize that she usually didn't.

"Power off your phones," she said, slamming the car door.

Matt pulled out his phone and asked, "Why?"

"You want it to tell your cell provider that there are two copies of it floating around? Or maybe you want to get last week's phone calls and texts? Spare yourself the headache, and switch it off."

He did, and so did Mason, slipping it back into his pocket.

"All right, boys, it's time," she said, and stepped around to the back of the car. "Let's get into the head space."

Mason stood with them and closed his eyes, clearing his mind, his heart pounding in anticipation, fearful that he might not be able to make it work. *You're good at this,* he told himself. *You've done it before.*

"Give me your hands, and focus your energy on me," she said.

Mason glanced around to make sure they weren't being observed, and the three of them stood in a circle, holding hands. Closing his eyes again, he concentrated on Hanh, then suddenly felt warmer. Hanh dropped his hand. The sun was streaming in the open sides of the parking lot. Hanh was grinning, and squinting in the new light.

"Fuck me," Matt said.

Mason looked out at the misty city below. Mostly to himself, he said, "Last Sunday morning."

Hanh set off decisively toward the hotel, her spike heels echoing on the concrete. As they moved to follow her, Mason glanced at the car—it had come with them, sitting there immutable, sunlight glinting off its windows. As they walked, he took his sunglasses out of his shirt and hung them on the outside of the pocket, the way Detective Kerr had.

The lobby made the place look expensive, even more than in the photo Mason had seen, trendily decorated in black and polished metal, the furniture in dark wood and purple fabric. Crystal lamps hung from the ceiling, and cozy alcoves housed candlelit tables and black-upholstered seating. As Effie had told him, it was quiet today, with only a handful of people around.

"Swanky," Matt said.

Mason nodded. "It's the best hotel west of St. Louis."

"That may be a tiny little bit of hyperbole."

Hanh stopped once they were inside and turned to them, her expression serious. She grabbed each on them firmly by the forearm and spoke formally.

"Go forth, young ones, and know that my heart is with you on your mission."

Mason could only stare at her, taken aback by the gravity of her words.

She released her grip and added more casually, "Come and find me in the bar when you're done." With that she walked away, disappearing around a corner.

"Do you get the feeling that we're totally working for her now?" Matt asked, watching her leave.

"My sense of it is that we don't have to if we don't want to. In a way I actually feel like I've been promoted—she had me come up with this plan on my own. So maybe we're collaborators rather than flunkies."

"That's reassuring." He turned and looked Mason over. "Are you ready, Agent Orange?"

"The name is Agent Rutherford," Mason said irritably, and walked toward the front desk, where a lone client stood chatting with the clerk, luggage stacked nearby.

"Where did that name come from?" Matt said, catching up and walking abreast. "It was on the tip of your tongue when I asked."

"It's an old family name," Mason said, and then inhaled sharply. "There she is." That curly blond haircut was unmistakable. She was farther down the lobby, sitting alone at a desk and staring into a computer screen. There were no other staff stationed nearby, he noted with relief, and the client chairs in front of her desk sat empty.

"Here we go," Matt said, and they strode purposefully toward her.

Effie definitely looked the part, her jacket a shade of almost-black violet that matched the hotel's decor, with a white blouse and a tag on one lapel that bore her name. Her earrings were the same cartoonish plastic buttons she always wore, today in a shade of purple.

She glanced up at them as they approached. "On your honeymoon, boys?" she said cheerfully. "Sit down, we'll find you something fun to do."

"What?" Matt said. "No."

Mason hesitated, thrown off for a second, but then found his footing. "Are you the psychic?"

Effie's eyes narrowed. "No, I'm the concierge. Do you need a psychic?"

Matt had his phone in hand, peering at the black screen. It was still powered off, but Effie couldn't see that. "Athletic blond. That's her," he announced, and palmed the phone.

Mason put his hands on his hips, trying to look intimidating. "Effie Brownstein. We've been looking for you."

Effie shrank back in her chair, her eyes growing wide. "What? Who are you?"

Mason pulled out his ID wallet and held it open toward her. She leaned across the desk to read it, and Mason quickly flipped it closed and pocketed it.

"The Office of Psychic Conformity?" she said. "Is that federal? I've never heard of it."

"That's because you're not working as a psychic, even though you have the power. If you were a psychic for pay, you'd know all about us," Mason said, and added, "every which way from Tuesday, lady."

Matt shot him a look: *tone it down.*

Effie looked alarmed now. "You seem to know a lot about me."

"We know about the déjà-vu thing," Matt said, his tone conciliatory, "and we know it's not something you can control."

"Still," Mason said harshly, "you have to play by the rules."

"What rules?" Effie said, looking from one to the other. "What are you talking about? Am I in trouble?"

"Should you be?" Mason demanded.

Matt put his hand on Mason's arm, as if to hold him back. "You're not in trouble," he said to Effie. "Not yet. May we sit?"

"Of course," she said, waving distractedly to the chairs in front of them.

Once they were seated, Mason pulled his chair closer to the desk and leaned toward her. He spoke quietly, but held her gaze.

"Later today, when Elmer's watching the football on TV—"

"You know Elmer?" she asked, her tone rising.

"Charming guy," Matt said casually. "He's smart—keeps his nose clean."

"Maybe you don't know him," she said.

"We know you're planning to drive up to Ojai today, to visit the orchard," Mason said intently.

"I was just thinking about doing that. But—"

"Just listen," Mason insisted. "You're going to have a premonition about splintering, where your energy fractures, like splitting an apple, or the segments of an orange. Then, when you're in the orchard and focused on the trees, you'll see the opportunity to do it. It'll be very tempting, but you have to resist the urge. It'll cause problems for you and a lot of other people. Just let the feeling pass."

"How do you know all this?" she asked, staring at Mason in wonder.

"It's our job, Effie," Matt said, drawing her gaze. "Psychic conformity."

"She gets it, Smith," Mason said. "She's a smart lady."

"And attractive," Matt said.

Effie reacted visibly, recoiling in surprise.

"You know there's more going on in this world than your regular senses perceive," Matt said, affecting an intimate tone. "It's fine to go up to Ojai, and it's fine to reminisce about the orchard, but don't splinter. Conforming is simple, like Agent Rutherford said."

"OK," Effie said, nodding.

"We won't bother you again," Matt continued, "unless …"

"I get it," she said. "Don't splinter."

She seemed to understand what he meant, Mason thought. Maybe she'd already had the premonition.

192

"Good answer," Mason said, and sat back, as if he was tired, and rubbed his eyes. "You know what they say, Effie. When your Uncle Sam says jump ..."

"You jump," she said softly.

Mason stood and turned to leave.

Before Matt joined him, he said, "Have a pleasant afternoon, ma'am."

When they were halfway across the lobby, Mason said, "Nice touch."

"Don't look back," Matt hissed. "She'll totally be watching us." Once they had walked the length of the lobby and were out of sight, around the corner and inside the bar, he said, "High five, man."

Mason slapped his hand, elated. "Yeah!"

"It totally worked."

"I know, right? You could see it in her eyes. I wonder, though—should I tell her about the boat? Like, 'Stay away from the edge.'"

"Oh, fuck, no," Matt said. "You think things are messed up now? That would be a recipe for disaster."

"Maybe I could just tell her 'Beware of high places,' or something generic."

Hanh, perched on a barstool, turned as they approached. "Please tell me you didn't say anything like that."

"Misguided, huh," Mason said.

"Extremely. From your testosterone-fueled hand-slapping I assume it went well?"

"It went great," Matt said. "I could hear her heart pounding from across the desk."

"I think she got the message," Mason added.

"Then let's go," she said, and slurped at her martini glass, pulling the olive off the toothpick with her teeth and chewing it as she slid off the barstool. She pushed her change across the bar and called, "Thanks, Rosa," waving briefly to the bartender.

Walking out, Mason looked into the lobby, but couldn't see Effie. In the parking structure he scanned the space to confirm they were alone, and once they reached Hanh's car, she waggled her fingers for them to join her. He could almost feel it as it happened, feel the energy crackling, when he linked hands with them. Before he could even close his eyes the sky flashed orange, and it was night.

"Home again," Hanh said, as blasé as if they had just stepped off the metro.

Mason stood for a minute to get grounded, reoriented to the here and now. He powered on his phone and followed Matt into the car, letting him climb into the back this time. Checking his phone, he was relieved to see that the date was correct, but he noticed that it was after one. They hadn't been in the hotel more than half an hour. That didn't seem right—it felt like they were being shortchanged on time. He decided not to ask Hanh about it. Maybe that's just the way it worked.

Hanh drove down the ramp and out onto the street. Mason was exhausted, and his companions were similarly subdued. He closed his eyes and leaned back on the headrest. *Thanks, little car,* he thought, sending the words outward with his mind. *Thanks for whatever part you played in this.*

194

The high-pitched whine of the tires moving fast on concrete lulled him into semiconsciousness, and he felt himself sinking into the hypnagogic state, the seeds of dreams intruding on his mind. He was in a dark office then, computer monitors filling two walls, full of graphs, tables of numbers, and surreal mottled black-and-white photos. No, not photos; they were moving—video feeds. Two men, sullen but attentive, wearing uniforms like Ortiz's, sat at a desk, illuminated only by the monitors. Those haircuts—they were definitely military guys. One of them had a keyboard and the other sat in front of a joystick, like he was playing a video game.

They had no idea he was here, watching their monitors, one of them intermittently tapping on his keyboard. Surely they would have seen him by now. He was close enough to reach out and touch the guy on the arm. But he wasn't here, he realized, not really, at least not with his body. They were never going to notice him. Stepping closer to the desk, he peered at the lowest monitor, an image of blue-gray watercolor paints spilling down the screen. It was slowly drifting horizontally, like a close-up pan across a vast artwork, and Mason became mesmerized, watching the monochrome wash pattern slide by. The screen was studded with hair-thin black plus signs, he saw as he looked closer, evenly spaced and unmoving, the gray sliding past underneath them. The display above it was more colorful, constantly changing numbers plotted on a circular graphic that rolled at the same slow pace as the watercolors.

"Look at this," the one with the keyboard said, and Mason focused on him again. He was pointing at the screen with the watercolors. A point glowed bright white amid the gray.

"What the hell?" the other one said.

"Let's get a closer look."

Mason watched them, their faces shifting from boredom to concern, the one with the joystick intently manipulating it now. Turning back to what they were looking at, the gray screen juddered, reversing direction, and shifted to something else: a solid gray field studded with irregular black dots, the point of white light now on a line running through the middle of it.

"It's on a highway," the keyboard jockey said, leaning toward the screen. "Get closer."

On the screen the image shifted again, an overhead view of a ribbon of asphalt winding through the empty black-and-white desert. That's what he'd been looking at all along, he realized, the desert from high above, surreal in blues and grays because it wasn't a visible-light image, it was something else. The screen panned to the left and a bright blob came into view, scintillating at the edges.

"It's moving," the one with the joystick said. "What spectrum is that?"

"Gamma rays," the other said grimly. "Whatever it is, it's unshielded. If that's a vehicle, the driver should be fried."

"What about X-rays?"

He clattered on his keyboard for a second and the

image changed, a dark boxy shape traveling serenely along the highway.

"Nothing," he said. "Try visible light."

The image shifted again, and Mason knew now what he was looking at: Hanh's beat-up little car, seen from above, the windows perfectly clear, the angle of the image revealing a set of hands on the steering wheel—Laura.

"Call the eggheads," the joystick jockey said. "There's someone in that car."

This wasn't a dream, Mason realized. He was being shown the incident that got Laura detained and taken to Area 51. He was in that same car right now, he realized with a start, and woke up.

Hanh was off the freeway, on Sunset just a few blocks from Pretty Nail Blowout. He blinked and focused on retaining the image of the little room, the military technicians watching her car on monitors. *Drones,* Laura had said. They were drone pilots. It didn't feel like a dream that he needed to go over in his mind to remember. It was already rooted there, more like a dreamy memory. Where had that come from?

They pulled into the parking lot at Pretty Nail Blowout, and Mason watched Hanh as she shifted into park and switched off the ignition.

Was the insight from her? No—more likely it was the car that had shared the scene with him. It was something an acquaintance would do as a favor, he thought, providing background information like that, and he and the little car were certainly well acquainted with each other after their lengthy desert road trip.

He and Matt said good-night to Hanh and walked back toward Matt's vehicle, Mason hugging himself in the cold.

"What's so funny?" Matt asked, eyeing him.

"Not funny," he said. "Just happy. I think I made a new friend."

eleven

On Sunday he got his hair cut in preparation for appearing in front of Iris's television cameras, then joined Ned at his parents' house for their traditional post-mass lunch. Ned's mother had never heard of *America's Filthiest People,* but his father had, using a Spanish word to describe it that they all eventually agreed translated as "stomach-churning." Mason tried to go to bed early, as his ride was coming at 6:15, but he lay there for a long time, restless, his body not amenable to the sudden revision in his sleep pattern.

He didn't put a lot of thought into what he wore, as none of the regulars on the series seemed to dress up—the subject was filth, after all—and he picked a bland pair of khakis and a gray polo shirt. Bleary-eyed, he managed to down a couple of pots of espresso before his ride arrived. He didn't wake Ned before he left.

As he walked outside, the driver stayed in the town car, idling in front of the garage, exhaust billowing dramatically in the cold morning air. Mason opened the back door and climbed in.

"Mr. Braithwaite?" the driver asked, eyeing him in the rearview mirror.

"That's me."

"We'll be there in forty minutes."

"Thanks," Mason said, and settled in, gazing out the window as the car started down the hill.

"I don't recognize you," the driver said, pulling his attention back. "What shows have you been on?"

"None of them," he said. "I'm doing a guest appearance today."

"Oh, yeah," the driver said, looking back to the road, clearly disappointed, and left him alone for the rest of the ride.

This was the second time in a week he'd been out at this hour. The city looked weird, all gray and blue in the breaking early light. He didn't have the energy to read the news on his phone or even check his email, so he watched the streets, then the busy freeways. Finally they pulled up at a little suburban house with a deep lawn in front. Most of the street was quiet, but two location trailers were parked out front, half a dozen people were milling around the yard, and the front door to the bungalow hung wide open.

Climbing out of the car, he could see inside the house. It looked just like others on the series: all manner of valueless stuff, paper and plastic, food containers and clothing, boxes and bags, essentially all trash, piled deep and stretching as far back as he could see.

He stood there taking it in for a second, until he heard his name called. It was Iris, standing by one of the location trailers. She was dressed in blue and white and green, color blocks on her body like the flag of some new nation.

"Good morning," she said cheerily, squeezing his arm. "You look a little sleepy. There's coffee inside."

She was truly a morning person, he realized. Compared to her afternoon persona, to his eyes right now she appeared to be operating in fast-forward.

"It won't help," he said. "But I'll wake up soon enough."

"I want you to meet the production accountant," she said. "She's just inside."

Mason followed her up the steps into the cramped trailer, where a woman in half-frame glasses sat at a little table with a laptop, surrounded by stacks of paper, a printer, and a coffee urn.

"Paperwork," Mason said.

"That's me," she said, and Mason spent a few minutes with her, filling out a tax form, something called a guest-star contract, and an image release. That document was three full pages of dense text, and scanning through it, he found that it entitled the production company to use his image anytime, anywhere, for any reason. It was broad and sweeping language, but it was probably standard, so he signed it and handed it back.

"We're going to 1099 you in January," the accountant said, looking at him over her glasses.

"I'd expect no less."

"This is the NDA," she said, handing him another multipage document. "It's the most important one. You can read it, but basically it says you can't disclose our production techniques or work styles to anyone."

"I get it," Mason said, flipping to the last page and signing it. He couldn't imagine anyone would even care about such esoteric minutiae, or that he'd even want to retain it.

After he'd surrendered the last sheaf of paper, he went back outside, ducking to exit the trailer's low doorway. Iris was gone, but a young man with bushy hair and a ball cap, holding a clipboard, was standing there on the sidewalk, and caught his eye.

"I'm Mike," he said with a smile. "I do postproduction."

Mason introduced himself and asked, "What does postproduction entail?"

Mike frowned. "Editing the video, adding the titles, smoothing out the sound, that kind of thing. You're not in the industry, huh."

"I'm the psychic."

"I thought you looked familiar," he said, his brow furrowing. "Were you involved with that Billy Blood soft drink guy? He hired a psychic."

Mason nodded. "Tyler Frey. I worked for him very briefly."

"I remember that story in the news," Mike said. "That guy went down in flames."

"I wouldn't know anything about that," Mason said, even though he'd been instrumental in bringing down Frey's corrupt enterprise.

Iris walked up and put her hand on Mason's shoulder. "You need to get into wardrobe."

"Of course," he said, moving to follow her. "Nice to meet you, Mike."

Iris led him into the other end of the trailer, a claustrophobic closet lined with double racks of clothing stretching floor to ceiling. A curvy woman with her hair pulled back stood inside. He hadn't anticipated the need to change clothes; clearly the televised version of reality was subject to wardrobe adjustment.

"Sofía will help you get dressed," Iris said, and left.

Sofía assessed him for a minute. "Can you do a little twirl?" she asked.

He dutifully turned in a circle and stopped to face her with what he hoped was a quizzical look.

"I think we'll do a tweed jacket and denim," she said finally. "That seems psychic."

"I don't usually wear jeans. They're too hard to cycle in."

"You're not cycling now," Sofía said, grinning at him. "Besides, it's the official fabric of California. It's almost your duty to wear it at some point."

"Fine," he said. "Jeans it is."

"What's your size for trousers?"

"I don't know, but it'll be on the tag inside these pants. Can I just take them off here?"

"You don't know your own pant size?" she said, incredulous.

"I don't spend a lot of time focused on clothes."

She nodded. "I can see that. Well—let's drop trou, bro, and see what we have to work with."

Ten minutes later he was wearing a pair of jeans, which didn't fit too badly, he had to admit, along with a white dress shirt and a tweed jacket, even a pair of brown saddle shoes that matched the outfit. After he'd pulled on the jacket, Sofía insisted on tying a dark-red bow tie around his neck.

"It makes you look like a specialist," she said, pulling the door closed and stepping aside so that he could see himself in the mirror on the back of it. "You look like you know what you're doing."

"I guess there's something to be said for that. Thanks, Sofía."

Another staffer was waiting for him when he stepped outside. "I have your mike," she said, and spent a minute with him on the sidewalk, attaching it to his lapel and threading the wire through his shirt to a battery pack that she attached to his belt in the small of his back.

A scruffy-looking woman with gray hair came up to them. She must be freezing, Mason thought, wearing a hot-pink blouse in a billowy thin fabric, and wondered fleetingly if she was homeless, wandering over to see what all the activity was about.

"I'm told I'm next to get miked," she said. "Are

you the psychic?"

"Yes—I'm Mason," he said, slipping his jacket back on.

"Nice to meet you. I'm Mary-Beth."

"OK," he said, and frowned.

She lifted her arms as the technician worked on her mike.

"I'm the crazy person whose house this is," she explained.

Mason's eyebrows shot up. "Oh—I get it. Nice to meet you too, Mary-Beth."

She grinned at him. "You seem surprised. You were expecting someone filthier?"

"No, no. I guess I'm just feeling a little weird about this whole experience. I watch the show, but my roommate refuses. She says it's exploitative."

"I won't ask you what they're paying you," Mary-Beth said, "but I'll bet there's an extra zero on your check from what you usually get paid, right? Mine too. It'll help me clean up this place, put some new carpeting down, and sell the house."

"You're ready to go," the technician said, and walked away. Mary-Beth dropped her arms.

"I'm glad you feel that way about it," Mason said. "It's not exploitation if you're getting fairly compensated."

"I'm not sure that's true," she said, frowning. "Still, I'll be able to move to some nice retirement village in Florida. There are too many memories for me in LA. I'm done with all the flaky people here."

"Of course," Mason said, raising his eyebrows.

"It's easy to write us off if you've met all ten million of us."

She frowned. "You working for the Chamber of Commerce or something, Red?"

"It's just that calling everyone in the whole metropolis a flake seems kind of irrational."

"Irrational? That's an interesting choice of words, coming from a psychic."

A woman with intricate dreads stepped up to them, putting her arm around Mary-Beth's waist and giving her a quick squeeze, smiling at Mason. She must have overheard them.

"You must be the psychic."

"Dr. Connie," he said. "It's such a pleasure."

"Ooh, honey, I'm no doctor. Only when the cameras are rolling. Just call me Connie."

"Got it," Mason said. "Connie it is."

She was shorter than she looked on television, he thought, and she'd changed her hair since last season, with some of her dreads dyed magenta. Her breezy manner was also nothing like the concerned and somber shrink she was on the series.

"I love what you've done with your hair," Mason said.

"Thanks," she said, grinning appreciatively and glancing at the trailer. "It was nice to meet you. If you'll excuse me, I need wardrobe to redo my corset."

Mason watched her leave, trying to decide whether she looked corseted or not, but he couldn't tell.

"So what is it exactly that I'm trying to locate in the house?" he asked Mary-Beth.

"My grandmother's precious necklace. It's set with forty-eight stones. I haven't seen it in years—not since she died. But I know it's in there somewhere."

"Do you have anything else that belonged to your grandmother that I could use to get insight? It has to be made out of metal."

"Sure, lots."

"It's best if it's an object that spent a lot of time with her. Another piece of jewelry that's not missing, maybe?" he offered.

"I think I know just the thing. I'll dig it out now, before we get started," she said, and walked purposefully toward the house.

Nearby, on the lawn, Mason spotted another familiar face, a guy with a trendy haircut and a prominent nose: Ray, the cleaner, dressed for manual labor in denim and a T-shirt. Mason went over and introduced himself, and Ray reciprocated with a toothy smile.

"I'm not sure if we have a scene together," Ray said, his dialect lilting New Orleans. "I haven't looked over the schedule."

"Is it really that planned out?" Mason said.

His eyebrows shot up. "Have you ever seen the show? The core elements are the same in every episode."

"I guess," Mason said. "But I thought for reality TV they'd just, you know, film it as it happens."

Ray smiled sympathetically. "Maybe our genre needs another name that doesn't have the word *reality* in it. It's misleading."

"Noddy," someone shouted, and Mason turned to see a thin, dark-complected guy looking at them from across the lawn.

Ray trotted over to him, and Mason saw that the guy's cap was embroidered with DIRECTOR in big white letters.

Iris appeared at Mason's elbow, her gaze fixed on Ray and the director, who addressed everyone in the front yard.

"This scene is Noddy's meltdown with Mary-Beth," he called. Mary-Beth appeared at the door to the house, and Ray stood with her, the cameraman hovering nearby, focused on the pair of them.

"Who's Noddy?" Mason asked Iris.

"That's Ray's nickname. Everyone calls him that. It's from some old-timey cartoon character. They say Ray's nose looks just like Noddy's."

While the director gave Ray and Mary-Beth detailed instructions, Mason pulled out his phone and did a quick search. The character was a cherubic elf with a red hat, and he didn't fill out a T-shirt quite as pleasingly as Ray, but his nose was similar, he decided, flipping through some images and then looking back at Ray to compare.

"Action," the director called, and as if a switch had been thrown, Ray instantly began berating Mary-Beth. She had tears in her eyes, Mason saw, which somehow must have happened before Ray lit into her.

"Mary-Lou," Ray screamed. "You've got to wake up—"

"Cut," the director called. "Start again. Her name is Mary-Beth."

"Forgive me," Ray said, grinning at her, and stepped back to await the director's cue.

"Mary-Beth, you've got to wake up. You need to choose between this trash and those babies. If you ever want to get custody back, you need to clean up this filth."

His Southern dialect was more prominent when he was shouting, Mason thought, unsure whether that was intentional or not.

"Cut," the director said. "Good work." Ray walked back toward the trailers, grinning and nonchalant, and the director conferred quietly with the cameraman.

"Why is he screaming at her when he hasn't even started the cleanup yet?" Mason asked, looking at Iris.

"It's filmed out of sequence," she said. "We wanted to shoot that scene outside, and the light is better in the morning."

Mary-Beth walked up to them, dabbing at her eyes.

"I didn't know about your children," Mason said to her. "I'm so sorry. Who has custody of them now?"

"Oh, god," Mary-Beth said, taken aback. "I don't have kids. That's just to add dramatic tension. Can you imagine children living in that mess?"

Mason glanced at the doorway to the bungalow, the mountains of clutter inside. "I could not," he said.

Nothing seemed to happen for a while, except people pacing around, sometimes conferring over tablet computers. Mason got a coffee from the accountant's office and lurked on the sidewalk, watching the inactivity.

Finally Iris strode up to him. "You're up," she said. "We're going to film the scene where you locate the necklace."

"I hope I'm going to locate it," he said, and followed her to the doorway of the house.

The director introduced himself and told Mason what he wanted. "You'll be talking to Mary-Beth. Explain concisely what you're going to do—you know, your psychic thing. Make sure you say her name. It's Mary-Beth," he said, raising his eyebrows.

"Got it," Mason said, nodding.

"Don't say 'um' and don't repeat yourself. Speak slowly. Look at her—don't look at the camera."

"OK," Mason said, less confident now, trying to absorb it all.

"Just act natural, as if the camera wasn't here. You'll do fine."

None of those instructions were about acting natural, Mason thought, but he knew he could do this. The fact that they were amenable to shooting retakes made it feel like there was less pressure on him.

He stood where he was told to, on the lawn near the door and next to Mary-Beth, and waited while the camera got positioned. Eventually the director said, "Action."

"Mary-Beth," Mason began, looking at her and speaking as clearly as he could, "I'm going to try to locate your grandmother's necklace using a psychic skill called psychometry. To do that, I need to read something metal that once belonged to her."

Her eyebrows furrowed, and she thought for a moment. "I'm sure I can find something," she said, and went into the house, the cameraman walking in after her. A minute later they were back, and Mary-Beth held out a warped stainless-steel dog tag on a ball chain. He took it from her and examined it. It was a military ID tag with a man's name stamped on it, Percy Sutter, and below that a woman's name with an address in Lawndale. It was the address for this house, he realized.

"Who's Percy?" Mason asked her.

"My grandfather. He lived in this house."

"I actually need something of your grandmother's."

"Her name is on there too. She wore that around her neck for years after he passed, so it was hers." Mary-Beth put her hands on her hips. "That's what I've got."

"I guess I can try," Mason said, peering at the object in his hand.

"Cut," the director said. "That'll work fine."

"I still have to read it," Mason said. "Don't you want that on film?"

"We'll move inside for that," he said, signaling to the cameraman, who made his way through the front door.

"I'm pretty sure I can do it on the lawn," Mason said, glancing through the doorway. "It looks treacherous in there."

"For the cameras, it'll be much more dramatic to

have you inside," he said, and not waiting for a reply, called, "Action."

The cameraman was already inside, so Mason went through the door and climbed onto the mountain of trash, stepping gingerly to get his footing, the dog tag's chain swinging from his hand, taking a few steps toward the camera. It didn't smell as bad as he expected it to, probably because Mary-Beth didn't keep rotting food like some of them did. Still, it was redolent of trash, and standing in here was like walking past a Dumpster rather than climbing into one.

He bumped his head on the ceiling and realized it was easier to walk if he braced his hands on it for balance. The cameraman gave him a hand signal, his thumb and forefinger in a circle. He meant that it was OK to stop where he was, Mason realized with relief. Mary-Beth was just a few steps behind him, much more agile navigating her own filth.

"If you'll give me a moment, I'll try to get psychic insight from the dog tag," he said to her, enunciating clearly. He looked at the dog tag and carefully placed it in his right hand, piling the chain on top of it and covering it with his left, then closed his eyes. It was a struggle to get into the empty and receptive state of mind, being so precariously balanced on the hoard, stooping just below the ceiling, and with a video camera trained on him.

"Are you getting anything?" Mary-Beth asked.

"It'll take a minute," he said, not opening his eyes, and started again, clearing his thoughts.

The smell changed—he was getting the scent of

perfume, a flowery one, and felt he was standing with a woman, his arms around her waist, her hair in a 1940s style.

"Not you, Percy," he said aloud.

"You saw him?" Mary-Beth asked, excited.

"I think I *was* him," he said, opening his eyes. "I was dancing with your grandmother. She's a redhead, like me."

"She was," Mary-Beth said, her eyes growing wide. "That's her. I can't believe it."

"I'll have to go deeper," he said, holding her gaze, and for the benefit of the camera, "To do so, I must request complete silence."

"Of course," she whispered.

He closed his eyes again and felt the tag and the chain in his palm, focusing on a necklace, and not knowing what Mary-Beth's looked like, envisioned an archetypal necklace, Hanh's consensus concept of what a necklace was. The goal was to try to ascertain the direction it was in, to be able to point to it in the house. Nothing decisive came to him, but Mary-Beth had said it was set with forty-eight stones, so he focused on that image. Eventually he got a sense of where it was, and opened his eyes.

"Over there," he said, pointing to a corner of the room where the piles came within a few feet of the ceiling. "In a piece of furniture. A desk, I think, in one of the drawers."

"There is a desk in here somewhere," Mary-Beth said.

"I can point to it from outside as well," he said,

and followed her back to the doorway, thankful for the fresh air when he got onto the lawn, and thankful that he hadn't fallen in the trash.

They walked around to the side of the house, followed by the cameraman.

"It's just about here," Mason said, circling his finger toward a spot on the wall.

"That will help us a lot," Ray said, walking up to them, ignoring the camera but speaking clearly for its benefit. "We'll look for it when we get in there." He grinned at Mason. "You seem to have the gift."

"I guess we'll find out," Mason said.

Next, Ray and his uniformed cleaning crew of half a dozen people started digging through the house. Mary-Beth sat in a lawn chair near the door, and the cleaners laid out books and garments and anything else that wasn't undeniably garbage. Whenever a larger item, a piece of furniture or a lampshade or a ratty cardboard box, appeared in the hands of one the cleaners, Mary-Beth would shout, "I'm keeping that." Soon the lawn was densely piled with clothes, stuffed animals, boxes, and trash bags. It looked as if the house had vomited. Ray spent time with the camera following him, shouting directions at the crew, once coming out of the house and sinking to his knees on the lawn, gasping for breath.

"We found the refrigerator," he croaked. "It's been buried for years. There's a whole ecosystem growing inside."

Mason stepped farther away from the house, instinctively fearing contamination, and sat on the grass under a tree in a spot that he judged to be upwind from the bungalow's kitchen, near the trailers. He had to laugh—reality TV was nothing like reality.

twelve

After filming more of the cleanup process, the director looked around and asked, "Where's Connie?"

Someone jogged to the trailers to fetch her, and soon the shrink was making her way across the lawn.

"Is it time for my heart-to-heart?" she asked.

"Somebody get Connie a lawn chair," the director shouted.

Soon she was sitting with Mary-Beth, who had a box of old magazines on her lap, squinting at them in the bright sunlight. The camera watched them sitting there for a minute as she pulled out each magazine, reminiscing about the content: "Oh, this was a good one," and "I remember her," and "You can't get those anymore." She set each one in the "keep" pile beside her chair.

Connie spoke to her, using the evenly paced Dr. Connie voice that Mason knew from watching the series. "Mary-Beth, I know you're feeling a lot of guilt about neglecting your children, and having them taken away from you. But hanging on to these magazines won't replace those babies. You're suppressing a lot of hurt. You need to feel it to heal it."

Tears ran down Mary-Beth's cheeks, and she heaved with silent sobs, clutching a tattered magazine tightly to her chest.

"Let it out," Dr. Connie said, massaging her back.

As the scene unfolded, and then as the director discussed punching it up for the retakes, Ray walked over to the side of the yard where Mason was. Mason got up to greet him.

"I thought you'd need an ambulance after you found the fridge," he said.

Ray laughed. "It was pretty bad, not even exaggerating for the camera."

"Do you just throw out the whole thing?"

"That wouldn't be very entertaining. We make her go through it and pull everything out first."

Mason nodded. "I guess that's why we watch."

"So, do I detect a little flair in your step, Mason?"

He looked at his saddle shoes. "They're from the wardrobe woman. I don't really know anything about fashion or brands or any of that."

Ray grinned. "That's not what I mean. I'm asking you if you're gay."

"Oh—well, your gaydar is calibrated correctly. I am."

"Do you want to make out?"

"Wow," Mason said, surprised. "I did not see that coming."

"Well?"

"Here?" he said, looking around. "Aren't we working?"

"Why not here? We're on a break."

"It doesn't matter anyway. I can't."

"You can't because you have a cold sore?" Ray said, raising his eyebrows, "or you can't because Jesus is watching? Or is it because you don't want to?"

"Of course I want to," Mason said. "Look at you—you're hot. And you're always firm but fair with America's filthiest people. That's laudable. But I'm with someone, and we're exclusive."

"Is he on set?"

"No, man," he said, gesturing to the crew. "This isn't my world."

"So he won't ever know," Ray said, grinning now.

"But I'll know."

Ray sighed. "Your loss."

"I'm curious," Mason said, meeting his eye. "Does that line usually work?"

"About half the time, I'd estimate. No one expects it unless you're at a nightclub, so it has that impact—*bam.*"

"Indeed it does," Mason said.

"And you, my friend, are missing out on the power of the Noddy."

He walked away, completely unfazed, before Mason could reply. It made no sense that Mason was the one who was embarrassed, heart pounding. He ran his fingers through his hair, then went to get a coffee from the urn in the accountant's trailer.

Iris found him soon after. "We need you to do the necklace reveal scene," she said.

"Did they find it?" he asked.

She nodded, grinning at him, eyes bright.

"Excellent," he said, beaming like an idiot. As they walked back toward the bungalow, he put an arm around her shoulder and squeezed.

"It's almost like you didn't expect them to find it," she said, looking at him sidelong.

"It's not that. It could have gone either way. I'm just happy I was right."

Mary-Beth was standing outside the front door, holding a sparkly loop in hand. Nothing like what he'd imagined, the stones were huge and not set, instead linked together by a tarnished silver chain. It looked cheap, even plasticky—definitely costume jewelry. On the grass nearby, just outside the front door, sat a low chest of drawers, battered and stained, the drawers haphazardly ajar.

"Rolling," the director said, and Mason stood with Mary-Beth.

"I found my grandmother's precious zirconium necklace," Mary-Beth said, holding it up so it sparkled in the sunlight. "No thanks to the psychic, though," she added, eyeing him. "It's very lucky that we checked that drawer."

"I said it was in a drawer," Mason said, more sharply than he'd intended.

"You said it was in a desk. It was in a dresser," she said, her tone accusatory.

"That doesn't mean I'm wrong. Was it in the right place? The same part of the room that I pointed out, at least?"

Dr. Connie stepped between them, and spoke to Mason in her gentle caring shrink voice. "Mason, we know you've got your own issues to deal with. Today is about helping Mary-Beth."

Mason could feel his face heating up. "I don't have any issues. I'm just defending my work. I'm not wrong, and I'm not crazy. The crazy one is right behind you," he said, pointing at Mary-Beth. "Look inside her house."

"Now, Mason," Dr. Connie said gravely, "we don't use that kind of language. It's labeling. Mary-Beth has a disease. It's called hoarding disorder, and she can't help it."

She was speaking in the therapist's voice she used on the show when people were at their craziest and most volatile, he realized, but he couldn't call her on it, not with the camera on them.

Mary-Beth spoke, tears streaming down her face. "It's just so hard. He was in there, stepping on my stuff."

"It's not like I damaged anything," Mason said. "I was standing on three feet of trash."

Mary-Beth sobbed. "You damaged my stuff with your dirty feet, and by looking at it with your lecherous psychic probing."

Dr. Connie comforted her with a hug. "Focus on the success, Mary-Beth. You found the necklace, even if it wasn't through psychic power. Take the win and move on."

Mary-Beth wiped the tears from her face and held up the necklace in both hands. "You're right," she said. "I found it."

Connie spoke to her a little longer, and Mason stood there, watching them, extremely uncomfortable, blood pounding in his ears. They were making him look incompetent. *You're getting paid well for this,* he reminded himself. Focusing on that helped him calm down. Finally the director called the scene, and Connie walked off. Mary-Beth quickly recovered her composure.

"You're very good," Mason said to her.

"Thanks, honey," she said, smiling at the compliment and twirling the necklace around her finger, then sauntering back inside.

The cleanup process wore on, and Mason couldn't tell how much of it was real and what was meant for the camera. Mary-Beth sat in her lawn chair, sorting her possessions.

"I need footage of the psychic," the director called, and Mason walked over to him. "Stand there and watch the sorting process," he instructed, and Mason did, hands on hips, surveying the work.

"Let's get you in the living room," the director said, and Mason obediently walked inside.

A lot of the trash was gone, and he could walk on

the now visible carpeting, so stained and dirty that he couldn't tell what color it was supposed to be. The smell had changed too—it was sharper, and stuck in his throat.

"Give me shocked and impressed," the cameraman said, training the lens on him.

"At the same time?"

"Or in series. Whatever you can do."

Mason stood and surveyed the room, projecting the requested emotions as best he could, trying not to wrinkle his nose at the smell.

"That should do it," the cameraman said. "Get out while you can still breathe."

The sun was low in the sky when the director finally called the crew together and announced the last scene.

"Mary-Beth, Ray, Connie, and the psychic, in that order, I want you to walk into the living room. Show me how blown away you are, how happy you feel."

Instead of walking into the bungalow, the entire crew trooped across the lawn toward the tree Mason had been sitting under, then onto the neighboring lawn. The front door stood open on this house as well.

"What are we doing?" Mason asked Iris, walking along with everyone.

"Do you see how similar they are?" she said, gesturing to the two houses. "The whole neighborhood is 1940s tract homes. This one is an exact copy, so it can stand in as the cleaned version of Mary-Beth's house."

The cameraman went in first, followed by the director, who soon called "Action."

Mary-Beth walked inside, and Mason could see her reaction through the door, her hands shooting up to clasp her mouth in shock. Then the tears flowed. "It's so beautiful," she said. "I have my life back. My babies can come home."

Dr. Connie followed her in and gave her a hug. When it was Mason's turn he walked in to find the room completely empty save for a few pieces of furniture. The carpet was pristine, and a table had a vase of fresh flowers on it.

"Wow," Mason said, looking around.

"Cut," the director snapped. "You weren't amazed enough. Let's try again."

Mason stepped outside, blushing.

Iris spoke encouragingly. "Imagine you're seeing Mary-Beth's house as clean as this one is. Wouldn't that be startling?"

"Nothing short of miraculous," he said. "I think I can do that."

He took a deep breath and walked back inside, stopping and gawking at the room in wonder.

"Oh, my god," he said under his breath, slack-jawed. "It's so … clean." He thought it might be too much, but the camera kept rolling. Stepping over to Mary-Beth, he said, "You've done it, Mary-Beth. You can start your new life."

She hugged him around the waist, tears shimmering in her eyes.

They spent a few more minutes for the camera

surveying the room, and then the kitchen and the bathroom. Eventually they were finished, and the director told everyone, "That's a wrap."

"You did great," Iris said, walking with him back to the trailers. "I'll let you know when we have a rough cut to look at."

"It's been fun," he said. "As a viewer, though, some of the magic may be gone."

She grinned. "Even so, don't stop watching."

After he'd changed back into his own clothes in the wardrobe trailer and surrendered his mike, he found a town car waiting for him, and told the driver where he lived.

The first thing he did when he got home was to take a long hot shower, washing away the memory of all the garbage, the dust, and that smell. Ned made dinner for them, a mushroom and bell pepper stir-fry, and Mason told him all about his day.

After they'd cleaned up their dishes, Ned said, "Are you up for more trash? There's a new episode of *Pica Confessions*."

"Oh, hell, no," Mason said adamantly. "No reality TV for me. Not for a while."

Instead he went into the office to Ned's bookshelf and found a dog-eared volume about mythology, taking it out to the sofa, where he read until bedtime, getting lost in the grand tales of the ancients.

Climbing into bed with Ned, he drifted into sleep almost instantly, and found himself in the dream state. He was in a temple, the classical kind he'd been envisioning when reading about Greek mythology, but the floor was wildly uneven, with big gaps in places, like climbing boulders in the Mojave. It smelled bad here, he thought, walking precariously on the boulder tops and hopping among them, a smell like ammonia and vinegar and chemicals and rot—enough to make him nauseous.

Tuesday morning was so cold and overcast that Mason had no choice but to sleep late. Eventually he dragged himself out of bed to the kitchen counter, where he sat to eat bananas and mandarin oranges and sip his espresso. Ned and Peggy were gone, presumably working, and he was well into his second aromatic mugful, enjoying the feeling of waking up at his own pace, when his phone rang. It was a blocked number, but he picked up anyway: "Braithwaite."

"It's Detective Kerr."

"Hey, detective. How are things down on the docks?"

"Have you spoken to Effie Brownstein lately?"

"Not since that day at Beth Israel. Is she missing?"

Kerr snorted. "No, but Elmer Brownstein is in the hospital with six holes in him."

"What?" Mason said, setting down his mug. "He got shot? Is he going to survive?"

"The wounds were from a pellet gun, which isn't usually a lethal weapon, but he wound up in the hospital anyway."

"Who shot him?"

"I would love to know. I don't suppose you have any psychic insight?"

"None," Mason said, and hesitated. "Did you talk to Effie?"

"Neither one of them is saying anything. We decided not to hold her, but in my estimation, it's her—he pushes her off a ship, and she ventilates him. In my business we call it payback."

That term wasn't a police exclusive, Mason thought, but as much as he hated the idea, it made sense. "She's passionate, I know that much," he said. "But I really can't imagine her doing something like that."

"I can," Kerr said simply. "I see worse things happen every day." He cleared his throat. "Listen, Mason, you're the only person I've met who doesn't have a vested interest. Could you talk to her, and see if she'll get into it?"

"Yeah, I could do that," he said. "Although she's kind of my friend. Does that count as a vested interest?"

"You're the only one in their circle who hasn't immediately blamed one or the other. You seem to have an open mind when it comes to this pair. Maybe it's your psychic alternative lifestyle."

Mason wasn't sure if that sounded more like a compliment or an insult, but he let it go. "I'll see what I can find out. What hospital is Elmer at?"

"The same one as his wife."

After he ended the call he sat there, sipping his coffee, considering what to do. It would be easy to wash his hands of it, and not even call her. He wasn't beholden to Kerr, and he couldn't even contemplate the idea of ratting on Effie to the cops. No way was he going to do that. Still, he'd love to talk to her, and find out what had happened.

He'd check with his intuitive senses, he decided. At least that would give him an inkling as to whether he should avoid the matter entirely. Carrying his mug over to the sofa, he took a final sip and set it on the coffee table, then got comfortable, closing his eyes and clearing his mind. He thought about Effie, and seeing her in the hospital, and at the concierge desk. His awareness expanded outward, and he tuned in to whatever might seep in at the edges. He stayed with it for some time, and picked up a sense of darkness, or maybe it was heaviness, surrounding Effie. The woman was complex, but he got nothing that implied there was any threat to Mason.

Sitting up, he did a neck roll to bring his mind back to ordinary consciousness, then drained his coffee mug. Back at the counter, he dialed Effie's number and listened to her voice mail greeting.

"How are you doing with your recovery?" he asked the machine. "We should get together."

Ned had texted, he saw, sometime in the last few minutes:

Saw Hanh this morning; asked if you could swing by her shop.

What was he doing getting a manicure on a Tuesday morning, Mason wondered. More annoying was that Hanh couldn't just pick up the phone and call him. He could detour to Pretty Nail Blowout before he headed south. Checking the time, he sighed. It felt like this was going to be a long day.

Not relishing the thought of going out into the cold, he put on a T-shirt under a heavier fleece and a rain jacket for the afternoon's predicted precipitation, then put on long pants and tied his pant leg with a cycling strap. After he shoved a notepad into his backpack, he braced for the brisk air and pulled his wheels out of the garage. The sky looked ominous, but the streets were still dry, and he gradually warmed up with the effort of cycling along the boulevard toward Hanh's shop.

Tran was on the front desk and greeted him. "Hello, Mr. Mason. Ms. Hanh is in the back room."

"Thanks," he said, and flashed her a smile. Several of the staff, working with customers or otherwise, tittered as he walked through, but he brushed it off. It was a process, them getting familiar with him, and even though the reaction he evoked made him feel like a Sasquatch, at least one of them knew his name.

Hanh seemed happy to see him, offering him a coffee and then sitting at the table. One of the staffers was seated at the other end, eating her lunch, but she smiled shyly and ignored them, absorbed in her phone. Mason poured himself a mugful from the ancient carafe and sat with Hanh.

"Your solution seems to have worked, Agent Rutherford," she said.

"That's great news. How do you know?"

"Things have normalized."

"I'm so glad." He couldn't help smiling, glad for the success. "Would you and Laura have done it differently?"

"We're not the sole authorities on these things. It's important to have input from other psychics."

"So am I working for you now?"

Hanh laughed. "You're sharpening your skills, I would say, and expanding your repertoire. You should be happy."

"Oh, I am," he said, setting down his mug. "So is Laura still at Area 51?"

"I'm not sure," she said, shrugging. "It sounds like an interesting place."

"Not the part I saw. It was just a dusty worn-out military base. I didn't get to go ogle the saucers."

"I'm sure we'll hear all about it someday," she said.

They talked for a while longer, and Mason enjoyed engaging with her more than he ever had. Eventually he drained his cup and said good-bye, cycling back down Sunset toward the metro.

It really was a victory, he knew, not just successfully preventing Effie's incident but being entrusted with the whole undertaking. He was getting better at all this, he could feel it, even though it was hard to quantify. In any case it was an extremely positive development.

thirteen

An hour and a half later he was at the hospital in Long Beach, approaching the desk in the lobby.

"I'm looking for a patient named Elmer Brownstein," he told the clerk. "I'm his brother-in-law."

She clacked at her keyboard and studied the screen. "He's in 624."

"Do I need a pass?"

"Nope. Go on up."

That was a lot easier than getting into the ICU, he thought, as he rode up in the elevator, but as he passed the nurse's station, a guy in scrubs called loudly to him, "Can I help you?"

Mason stopped at the desk. "I'm looking for

Elmer Brownstein."

"The police said his wife wasn't allowed to visit."

"Do I look like his wife?"

He frowned, uncertain. "They said she was blond."

"Where's Elmer?" Mason demanded.

Disinterested now, the nurse looked away and gestured vaguely down the hall. "That way."

The rooms were clearly numbered, so it only took a minute to find it. When he got to the doorway he saw that it was a small single room, and Elmer was alone, staring sullenly into space. His furry shoulders were bare and his chest was bandaged, with an IV line running into one arm. The requisite array of monitoring devices surrounded the bed.

Mason knocked softly on the door frame, and Elmer smiled when he recognized him.

"It's the psychic," he said warmly. "How are you, man?"

"Doing better than you, clearly," he said, stepping inside.

"Sit down," Elmer said, waving to the chair.

Mason pulled it close to the bedside and sat. "So what happened?"

"Well, one of the pellets cracked my clavicle," he said, pointing to it. "I have thin blood, so I bleed a lot—it looked a lot more dramatic than it really was. I even drove myself here. They took me in right away—if you ever want to get into the emergency room in a big hurry, let me tell you, just show up in a white shirt drenched in blood. Really, though, I'm fine. It's nothing."

"Dude, someone shot you. It's not nothing." He glanced toward the door and asked quietly, "Was it Effie?"

Elmer's face hardened. "Did she send you?"

"I haven't seen her since she was in here. Three flights up, in the ICU."

Elmer nodded, satisfied with his response. "She's home recuperating after her incident. It's a shame—we had to eat the cost of those Cabo tickets."

"At least you're both alive."

"She can be a real harridan, you know? She has this hair-trigger temper, and when she loses it, all bets are off. Her eyes turn red, and she screams like a madwoman. You wouldn't recognize her—it's like a different person. She becomes this blur of rage." He twisted his hand in the air like a whirlwind, but stopped, wincing with pain at the exertion. "I just try to get out of the way."

"I haven't seen that side of her," Mason said. It was hard to believe she could act like that, but then again, Elmer was lying here riddled with pellet wounds.

"You're just a friend, so you wouldn't see it. It's reserved for loved ones." Elmer watched him for a moment. "It was nice to meet your boyfriend and your roommate the other night. I could tell you're all really decent people."

"Thanks," Mason said, surprised but pleased with the compliment.

"Can I trust you, Mason?"

"Sure you can." He grinned. "Although Detective

Kerr expects me to enlighten him if I find out what happened to you."

"That guy is a worse pain in the neck than getting shot."

Mason laughed. "You can understand, though, why he wants to know, can't you?"

"Sure, sure. Forget about him. I already have." He looked toward the door before continuing. "Confidentially, can I ask you a favor? There's no one else."

"You can ask," Mason said, watching him closely.

"Go to my apartment and get my passport and some cash out of my safe. I'm leaving the country."

Mason frowned. "Why can't you go yourself?"

"Because Effie's there," he said, his face contorted with frustration. "I'm whipped, Mason, and I'm man enough to admit it. I'm way too whipped to confront her. If I see her, it will all collapse back into our old patterns, and I'll never get away."

"Maybe you could slip in while she's at work."

Elmer shook his head. "She's off work indefinitely since her concussion. And I need to scram real soon. She likes you—you're one of the few people she'd let in. You could chat her up a bit, and then sneak into the office and get my stuff."

"Could I just ask her for your passport?"

"No, man, she'd freak out."

"Well, how am I supposed to get into your safe surreptitiously? It's not a very big apartment."

"You're the detective—you figure it out," he said, insistent. Then, more gently, "It's my only chance of getting out of here. Please."

"How about this," Mason said, thinking it through. "I want to talk to her anyway, so I'll go see her, and if the opportunity arises, I'll try to get your stuff."

Elmer sighed with relief. "That's all I'm asking."

Mason's phone rang, and he pulled it out and glanced at it. "It's her," he said, looking at Elmer.

Elmer's eyes grew wide. "Whatever you do, don't tell her you've seen me."

Mason nodded and stepped out into the hall to take the call. "Hey, Effie, how's it going?"

"Not well," she said. "Elmer's in the hospital."

"You two are not having a good week. What happened?"

"He's not badly hurt, but they won't let me see him. I'm still not steady on my feet, so it's probably just as well that I stay home. But I'm worried about him."

"I can understand that. Listen, can I drop by? I'm in Long Beach today."

"Of course," she said, her tone brightening. "It would be lovely to see you."

"Do you need anything?"

"Well, if you pass a supermarket, Sugar-Frosted Millet Clumps and a quart of soy milk."

"Millet clumps? That's a breakfast cereal?"

"Exactly. In the big blue box."

"Sure, I guess I can do that."

"If you're stopping anyway, maybe a bag of arugula. And a loaf of pumpernickel, and a nice heirloom tomato. Not those gross factory ones."

"OK," he said, grinning at her audacity. "See you in a while." He paused to type the shopping list into his phone before he went back into Elmer's room, dropping into the chair.

"Well?" Elmer demanded.

"It seems I've been invited to your apartment."

Elmer cackled. "Look at you, already working on it."

"I'll go over there today."

"That's my boy," he said, his eyes bright. "The safe is under the desk in the spare room. You can't miss it. It's easy to get into because it has a keypad. The combination is five-one-five-oh."

"Fifty-one fifty. That's easy to remember," Mason said, nodding.

"I know, right? Zubanski's jersey number when he was in college, fifty-one, and then in Albuquerque, fifty."

"That's football?"

"Of course that's football—the great Zubanski."

"Right. I was thinking fifty-one fifty, a psych hold."

"Is that one of your psychic techniques?"

"It's legalese for when the cops or doctors lock you in the psych ward if they think you're dangerous."

Elmer shook his head, as if trying to disperse that information before it took root and cluttered his mind. "There's twenty grand in cash—bring it all. It's still bundled, so it'll be easy to find."

"That's a lot of dough," Mason said. "Where do you work, again?"

"Never mind that," he said, jutting his chin out. "Where I'm going, I'll need it. And don't forget the passport."

"I'll try. I do feel a little bad giving Effie the runaround."

Elmer scoffed. "She'll never find out. And Mason, sincerely, thanks for doing this."

"Don't thank me yet," he said, rising from the chair. "I might not manage to pull it off."

"I'm sure you can do it," he said, nodding confidently. "And Mason—don't rip me off."

"I won't," he said, his face turning red. He moved to leave, but turned back when Elmer spoke.

"Also, Mason? Watch your back."

"Thanks," he said, and felt a shiver as he walked back to the elevators.

Unlocking his bike in the parking lot downstairs, his phone rang. The caller ID said it was Iris.

Picking up, he asked, "How's it going? Did my screen presence break one of your cameras yesterday?"

She laughed. "You were a natural, but I'm not calling about the show. I wanted to ask you to have coffee with me today."

"That's so sweet, but I'm down in Long Beach today, and I have to stop at a market …"

"What a coincidence. I'm in Long Beach today too."

"Even so," Mason said, "I don't think I have time. Let's do it another day."

"I really think we should talk before you head over to Effie's place," she said, dropping her breezy tone.

He froze. "How do you know about that?"

"Let me buy you a coffee, and I'll fill you in. It won't take long."

No one besides Elmer knew that he was on his way to see Effie, and he'd formulated the plan just minutes ago. It had to be some kind of psychic back-channel. He tried to sense it, feel what it meant, determine whether it was spurious or had gravity.

"This is important, isn't it," he said finally.

"Oh, yeah."

"Where do you want to meet?"

She gave him the name of a café. "It's in downtown Long Beach," she said. "I'll be there in a few minutes."

It was near the hospital, at least, he saw when he looked it up on his phone, and set off pedaling. It had rained while he was inside, but not a lot, as there were no puddles, and at least it wasn't raining on him now. The place was on a pleasant little street with wide sidewalks and public bike racks, so rare in his part of town. They were even the good kind that wouldn't mangle your spokes. After he locked up his wheels, he went inside, admiring the huge bright windows facing the street. The place wasn't busy, and Iris was waiting at a table with a coffee. She waved cheerfully when he came in. Today she was wearing a pastel color-block top, not jarring but still reminiscent of the rainbow. He acknowledged her with a nod, then ordered a double espresso at the counter before going over to join her.

"It's good to see you," she said as he sat down.

"I would say the same thing, except I don't know what the hell is going on." He threw his hands in the air. "How do you know I'm headed to Effie's place?"

Iris laughed. "Dude—chill. Catch your breath."

"Right," he said, sitting back. "The only explanation I can come up with is that you're psychic, or working with someone who's psychic."

"I dabble a little," she said, sipping her coffee. "I don't make a living with it the way you do, though, or create trouble like Effie did."

"How do you know about her?" he asked, and paused while the waiter set down his espresso. "Last week when we met in WeHo you couldn't even remember her name."

"In my parents' culture," she said, "they believe that people with psychic powers have bad luck. Conversely, people with good luck have no psychic abilities. If I came out to them as psychic, they'd think my life was over, that I'm going to wind up as a burden on them. So I keep it quiet."

"OK," Mason said, twisting his little cup on its saucer, hoping there was a point.

"That's why I never mentioned that I dabble."

"It also doesn't explain how you know about Effie."

"She's been in the news—falling off the cruise ship, and then today about Elmer getting plugged. It only makes sense that you'd be involved."

"No, it doesn't. You called me minutes after I decided I was going to her apartment. How did you manage that?"

"You of all people know there's information all around that's not obvious."

"Absolutely," he said. "But usually it's not about me, and most people can't obtain such precise details—especially information than only exists inside my head."

She sighed, and swirled the contents of her cup. "You know Effie isn't an ordinary person, don't you? She's straight out of mythology."

"That's exactly what she said about you," he said emphatically, louder than he'd planned. He glanced around the café, but none of the other patrons were paying them any attention. More quietly, he said, "Are you really some kind of Greek demigod?"

Iris laughed. "Of course I'm not. Gods and goddesses are a simplistic way of interpreting great truths. Ancient people crammed multidimensional stories into a framework they knew, even though the content is about the universal human experience."

"So you're not the Iris who visited the dark valley of sleep? The lair of Hypnos isn't in Lincoln County, Nevada?"

She smiled. "I'm the Iris who studied a lot of mythology in college and produces reality TV. I'm an ordinary person, but sometimes I have extraordinary experiences. You do too, don't you?"

"I do, that's true. Although I never went to visit Hypnos," he said, taking a long sip of espresso.

"When I was on that hike, I was vaguely aware that the symbolism of the journey was familiar. Effie just connected the dots more clearly."

"It's not just symbolic—it's exactly the same story. Iris visits the dark valley where the sun never reaches. You even said there were poppies growing in the canyon. Although the mythological Iris didn't hike to get there—she went in the sky, being the personification of the rainbow. Which is how you were dressed that day, by the way," he said, glancing down at her blouse.

"Walking up over that mountain range is a bit like traveling in the sky, isn't it?" She grinned. "It's such a great story. Personally, I didn't go there to ask Hypnos for a favor, but maybe I'm living it anyway, in a different way. I met you there, and then we worked together—psychic power and sleep are related, symbolically at least. Or maybe I got some inspiration or insight while I was there, or achieved something less tangible."

"That seems more plausible," Mason said.

"It's a common experience, probably happening all over the world all the time. The ancients just recorded it so that we'd remember."

"Effie knew Ovid's version. It mentions the poppies and the dark earth."

"There are versions of the story in lots of traditions, and lots of stories that resonate across cultures. The bear is a big one. Have you ever had a nightmare about being chased by a bear?"

His memory flashed to a recent dream, the fear he'd felt of a massive creature crashing through the woods. "Sure, something like that."

"It's hardwired into all of us, I think, and stories

about the great bear are widespread. In my grand-parents' mythology, the bear was at the center of the cosmos, even though the dragon gets all the name-checking."

He grinned. "Have you ever heard of the Pearl of Primordial Chaos in Chinese mythology? That's the name of the boat Effie fell off."

"It sounds familiar. I think maybe it's the origin of everything, like the kernel of the Big Bang."

"I don't know that much about mythology, but I've started reading a little. I figured I'd probably see more depth to the world if I learned about it."

"Shared stories permeate all our lives—the same echoes made by the same kinds of significant expe-riences. Even without knowing the classics, you can see how it happens in your own life. Think of a time when your experiences reminded you of someone else's story."

He thought of working with Matt on the dialog they had used on Effie, and making his Office of Psy-chic Conformity ID card. They had modeled them-selves on the pair from the Navy who'd come to the library, and used the same language. They had even approached her in the same way, appearing unan-nounced in a public place.

"I think I know what you mean," he said. "I just did something like that—modeled my own story on someone else's."

Iris sipped her coffee and waited for him to continue.

"I needed to motivate someone, so I recreated a

person who'd spooked me. It was an amalgam of a few different people, actually, but all with the same characteristics."

"What kind of person did you become?"

"Kind of an enforcer, like a plainclothes cop," he said. "I was trying to project the feeling of 'behave.'"

"I love it," she said. "Such an archetypal character. You can even summarize it in one word."

"True, but it doesn't really mimic a classical tale, does it?"

"How is you replicating someone else's story quantitatively different from an allegory?"

"Effie seemed to think you weren't even real—that you were only the allegory."

Iris scowled. "That's rich, coming from her. Did you ever ask her how she met Elmer?"

Mason had to think about it. "She said it was something about her last job, when she was running an orchard."

"Exactly. Remember how snobby she was about my farmers market apples?"

"I figured that was because she knew a lot about apples."

"Do you have your cell phone? Look up this story: Pomona the nymph."

"OK," he said, and fished it out of his pants, typing the name and then spending a minute reading. "She tended an orchard and wasn't interested in men. Vertumnus hangs around until he's able to talk her into falling for him, and then they work together." He looked up at her. "You think Effie is Pomona?"

"No, but I think her life has echoes of Pomona's story. If you say 'she is Pomona,' it becomes something solid and inflexible, which is useless. Solid things are impermeable, like isms. The point isn't that she's a mythological character, but that the character's story is a theme in her life—bleeding into it, reflecting a deeper universal truth."

He tucked his phone away. "I guess I can see that."

"Ask her when you see her today how she met Elmer, and tell me if you see any overlap."

"It's such a different way of looking at the world, and I love that alternative perspective. But Iris," he said, "why is it so important that we talk about this now?"

"Isn't it a great tool?"

"Anything that helps me understand the hidden complexity of the world is valuable, yes, so thanks for that."

"It also illuminates Effie, which is the timely part of why I wanted to see you. I want to come with you when you visit her."

"Why?"

She leaned toward him. "I can keep her distracted while you ransack the safe."

"I'm not going to do that," he hissed, and glanced around, hoping no one had overheard her. He watched her for a moment. "How did you know that's what I was going to do?"

"We have mutual friends in the psychic world."

"Hanh and Laura?" he said.

"Hanh, specifically. There was the suggestion

made that I help you out on this excursion."

"Why didn't you tell me before that you know her?"

"I didn't know that you knew her until this morning. And I told you about my parents—I'm on the down-low with the whole psychic thing."

"Right." He sighed. "I guess I shouldn't be surprised that Hanh knows what I'm up to."

"I don't think it's like a surveillance thing. It's more like she has a bigger range of information channels than we do."

"I'm blown away by how those two manipulate the world. They got the military to fly me to Nevada because Laura wanted me there, and then had them pay me for my time. But this is different—I literally just formulated this plan."

"Time doesn't mean much to them. Hanh probably heard about it from you next week, but she passed the information to me this morning."

"Before I even knew about it," he said, throwing up his hands.

She grinned, shrugging her shoulders, and drank the last of her coffee.

"It gets confusing," he said. "So you're not on their level, breezing through time like you were walking around the mall?"

"Not even close, brother. I'm a lot more like you."

"And Effie?"

"I'm not sure where she's at in her skills development. From the way Hanh explained it, I'd call her unconscious. Like lots of people, she has all this psychic power, and unlike most people, it's not suppressed, because she uses it, but she's mostly unaware of her potential."

Mason nodded. "That rings true. It's why I'm entangled with her." He drained his espresso cup and thought for a minute. "Why did we run into each other in the desert? Was that orchestrated by Laura or Hanh?"

"I didn't expect to run into anyone out there either, but I suspect it was arranged, yeah—and not just so you could be on *America's Filthiest People*. Maybe it was tangential to everything else that was going on. I'd wanted to make that trip, so maybe they nudged me somehow to do it that specific day."

"How well do you know Hanh?"

"We've helped each other out."

"Did you get in trouble, like I did? The pair of them basically rescued me."

"Not really," she said, her eyes narrowing. "It's more like a mentoring relationship."

That probably meant she was a more adept psychic than he was, he thought, or maybe she was just smarter.

"Was there a specific reason you were supposed to tag along today?" he asked. "I'm not sure I need help."

"It's up to you, of course," she said, shrugging and looking at her empty cup, "but our friend thinks you do, and I'm willing."

"I just wonder why Hanh thinks I need help? It's not a psychic logjam like Effie's thing. Why would she care about Elmer getting his passport?"

"I don't think it's about him—it's about you." She toyed absently with her cup. "This one time, I was moving a fridge with my boyfriend. We thought we could do it alone because we only had to get it up three or four steps. But it was too heavy, and we got stuck on the stairs. I was afraid I was going to break my back. Then this neighbor appeared. He'd seen us struggling, and he helped us get it up the steps."

"OK," Mason said. "Is this another allegory?"

"The point is, it's OK to accept help."

She was right, he knew. His resistance was just ego. He mentally pushed it aside and sat up in his chair. "So if you're coming with me to Effie's apartment, we should have a game plan."

Iris beamed. "What is it that you need to accomplish there, exactly? Just getting his passport out of the safe?"

"Right, but to do that, I have to get into the spare bedroom without Effie knowing what I've done."

"That sounds easy enough. How about this: We'll go in, be polite, chitchat, then I'll distract her, and you go break into the safe."

"I'm going to retrieve Elmer's passport for him, not break in," he said, appalled. "He gave me the code."

Iris raised her hands. "Whatever you say."

"How are you going to distract her?"

"I'll pick a fight. It's the best way to get someone's full attention."

"Really?" Mason said. "This is the woman who

allegedly capped her beloved husband—six times. Are you sure you want to provoke her?"

"An argument is perfect. She already resents me. You saw how she acted at the trailhead."

"Why would she resent you? She doesn't even know you."

"I have no idea. But I know it'll work." She grinned and stood up. "Let's go. I can drive."

fourteen

Mason followed her out to the street, and recognized her dark-red SUV, still grimy with the dust of the desert.

"Are you OK to leave your car?" she asked. "You're not parked at a meter that'll expire?"

"My car is a bicycle. It'll be fine."

"Oh, I'm so sorry," she said, her eyebrows shooting up.

"Don't be," he said irritably. "It doesn't mean I'm homeless."

She unlocked the car and went around to the driver's side, and Mason climbed in once she was behind the wheel.

"We have one stop to make," he said, as she

started the engine. "Any supermarket that's on the way to San Pedro."

"Why's that?" she asked, looking into her side mirror and pulling into the street.

"Does Ovid ever mention Pomona's personal assistant?"

She chuckled. "Not that I'm aware of."

"Well, I drove Effie across two states, and now I'm doing her grocery shopping. I feel like I'm acting out the parable of Pomona's PA." He waved his palm in the air, a slow wipe across the windshield. "Echoing through the millennia."

As Iris pulled into the parking lot of a supermarket, Mason checked the grocery list on his phone.

"Do you want me to come in?" she asked, pulling into a space. Tiny raindrops had begun to dot the windshield.

"Do you know what Sugar-Frosted Millet Clumps are?"

"Of course. 'Delicious complete nutrition for ages three to a hundred and three—with the goodness of high-fructose corn syrup.'"

He stared at her for a moment. "I can't believe you know that. I've never even heard of them."

"You should watch more television," she said, fishing a shopping bag out of the backseat and then climbing out.

"Let's split up," Mason said, trotting toward the entrance with her and hustling to get out of the rain. "If you can find the clumps and a loaf of pumpernickel, I'll get the other stuff."

Consulting the list again, he grabbed the items Effie had asked for and went to the register. Iris was already in line, and had a bottle of chardonnay in one hand.

"Wine?" Mason asked.

"We'll get Effie liquored up," she said simply. "It can't hurt."

The cashier scanned the pumpernickel and the chardonnay as Mason stepped up to the payment terminal.

"A loaf of bread, a jug of wine, and thou," he said, grinning at Mason.

Mason was occupied waving his phone over the terminal, trying to get it to connect, but he looked up. "Excuse me?"

"The bread and the wine," he said, reaching for the box of cereal.

"It's from Omar Khayyám," Iris said. "He was an eleventh-century Persian poet."

Mason nodded and eyed the cashier. "More classics I've never heard of."

The cashier shrugged. "I thought it was Shakespeare. You learn something every day."

"That is such a good attitude," Iris said emphatically.

"Omar Khayyám?" the cashier asked.

She smiled. "That's the guy."

Once they were in the car, Iris asked, "Where does Effie live, exactly?"

"I don't know the street, but I know the building," he said, and then remembered. "Wait—it's in my phone."

Finding the address in his navigation history, he set the phone on the console so that Iris could follow the map. He pointed out the parking spot Effie had had him use before, and they climbed out, Mason carrying the bag of groceries. In the lobby he scanned through the tenant list and pressed the button labeled BROWNSTEIN.

"It's Mason," he said when Effie answered.

The door buzzed open, and they got onto the elevator.

"You have to do a hard sell on the wine," Iris said. "It won't work if I do it."

"OK," Mason said, and took a couple of deep breaths, psyching himself up.

"No need to be stressed," Iris said. "It's just a social call."

He snorted and rolled his neck. Effie pulled open the door when he rapped on it, smiling broadly, but concern flashed in her eyes when she saw Iris.

"I remember you," Effie said, and gave her a little hug, then embraced Mason, kissing him on the cheek. "I'm so glad you're here. Come on in."

Mason set the grocery bag on the kitchen counter, looking down the hallway into the back of the house as he passed it. There were three doors, all of them open, with a folding door at the end, probably a linen closet. He knew already that one of them was the bathroom. One of the others had to be the spare room. His heart pounded at the thought.

"I brought some chardonnay," he called to Effie.

"I figured you could use a drink."

"Sure," Effie said, joining him in the kitchen. "Although I haven't really had dinner yet."

"I see wineglasses," he said, pulling three of them out of a cupboard. "Do you have a corkscrew?"

"I can do that, if you'd like," she said.

"You've had a rough week. Sit—I'll take care of it."

She pulled open a drawer to show him the corkscrew, then retreated. Mason poured three full glasses, and handed them to Iris and Effie, still standing in the living room, in front of the balcony door.

"Cheers," Iris said, and they clinked glasses.

Effie eased herself onto the sofa, still stiff from her fall, setting her wineglass on the coffee table. Mason picked an easy chair close to the hallway, setting his backpack on the floor beside it.

"It's nice to have greenery so high up," Iris said, looking out at the balcony.

"That's all Elmer," Effie said.

"And a lovely view of the port," she added, although the daylight was fading.

Mason murmured agreement. "So, Effie, last time I saw you, you said you didn't want to see Elmer again. What changed?"

"He's my beloved husband. You know that," she said, as if he were a bit simple.

"So why won't they let you go to the hospital?"

Effie scowled. "That awful policeman thinks I had something to do with putting him there. If I could just talk to him ..."

"Did you?" Iris asked.

"Talk to him? No. They've cut me off."

"That's not what I meant. Did you put him there?"

Effie arched her back, indignant. "We are *very* much in love," she said, and took a long drink from her glass.

"How did he wind up with all those pellets in him?" Mason asked. "Was he here?"

"Mason," she cried, "not you too. It's starting to feel like a conspiracy."

She wasn't going to say anything substantive about the matter, Mason realized. "You know, you never told me about how you two met."

"Didn't I? It was when I was running the orchard. I know we talked about that." She had a faraway look in her eyes. "Life was good, but it was a lot of work. I was busy. There was no time for men," she said, gesturing dismissively, as if it were trivial. "Elmer kept showing up, sometimes to work, or to deliver things. I was seeing him a lot. One day he was telling me this story, about the elm tree that was holding up the grapevine I'd planted. I had no intention of producing grapes, of course; it was just for fun, to see how they'd do. I realized then that he was more than just a friend—I was in love with him."

Iris shot Mason a knowing glance. It did sound a lot like the tale of Pomona.

"It's a lovely story," he said.

"It's so interesting that you think my story is straight out of Ovid," Iris said to her, "when you're clearly stumbling blindly through Pomona's life."

Effie turned to Mason, her voice rising. "You told her I said that? You didn't have to tell her that."

Mason shrugged helplessly.

"You've conned Elmer into playing your Vertumnus," Iris went on, leaning toward her, "and now you've shot him, and he's lying in a hospital bed across town."

"How dare you say that to me?" Effie shrieked. "I love that man more than life itself."

Mason was shocked at how quickly the conversation had turned acrimonious, but that had been the plan. "Can I use your bathroom?" he said, but they both ignored him, shouting at each other.

"You're the one stumbling through someone else's story," Effie said. "The dark canyon—*please.*"

Stepping into the hallway, Mason stuck his head into the first doorway, the master bedroom. The bed was unmade, with laundry strewn around, dishes piled on the nightstand. This is where Effie was recuperating. He moved on to the second door—this was the place. A fold-down futon sofa sat against the back wall, and under the window was the desk, really just a worktable with a file cabinet at one end. As he approached, he saw the squat black safe beneath it. He glanced toward the doorway, even though he knew he was alone; the heated voices were still back in the living room.

Tuning out their argument, he knelt in front of the safe and typed the code Elmer had given him into the keypad, 5-1-5-0. That was something Effie and Elmer could both benefit from, a psychiatric hold.

The number worked, triggering a soft mechanical *click* somewhere inside, and he twisted the handle, slowly so as not to make any noise, and pulled open the heavy door.

"You know nothing about my life," Effie shouted, her volume increasing, and Mason paused, watching the door, afraid that she might storm down the hallway, but Iris kept her there, talking now in a calmer tone.

The safe was piled with loose paper and folders—tax forms, letters, insurance documents—and a couple of jewelry boxes on top. He started digging through it and quickly found two bundles of cash, brand-new hundreds, he saw, still with their yellow bands on, as Elmer had promised, stamped with "$10,000." Pulling out another pile of paper, a heavy object tumbled to the carpet with a *thud.*

"Jesus," he said, under his breath, realizing with alarm that it was a handgun, ugly black with a silver trigger. Still in the safe was a clip, visibly loaded with full-size bullets—this was no pellet gun. He took a deep breath, grateful that he hadn't inadvertently fired a shot. He lifted the clip out of the safe using the papers underneath it, unwilling to touch it and put his fingerprints on it. If Kerr ever got hold of this, how would Mason ever explain that he'd been handling it? Thankfully Elmer hadn't asked him to bring that too.

Digging deeper, he found two passports. Flipping one open, saw that it was Elmer's, and pocketed it. He breathed a sigh of relief—he had what he needed, and Effie was still howling at Iris. Stuffing all the paper back in the safe, he spent a minute carefully sliding a manila folder under the pistol, cradling it with both hands, and gingerly setting it back inside. He hurriedly buried it under the rest of the paperwork, then silently closed the safe.

He should have brought his backpack in here, he realized; the cash bundles were the size of a brick, too bulky to go in his pants pockets. Realizing Effie and Iris had fallen silent, he turned to the doorway, stacks of cash in hand, his heart in his throat, but he was still alone. He needn't have worried, though, as Iris started haranguing once again.

"Why did you leave the fruit business, huh?" she demanded. "The real Pomona was able to stick with it."

"You're one to talk," Effie said. "Hiking eight miles across the mountains seems a lot like a fool's errand to me. What the hell did that prove?"

Mason stood there for a moment, considering what to do. Finally he stuffed the cash bundles into his underpants. It made his crotch look a little bulky, but it wasn't too obvious, he thought, smoothing the front of his trousers.

Breathing hard and trying to act calm, he walked back into the living room. Both women were on their feet, but at least there was some distance between them.

"We should go," Mason said, remembering to grab his backpack.

Iris relaxed her shoulders, visibly shifting gears.

"Effie, I'm sorry if I've upset you. I hope they let you see your husband." She moved toward the front door.

"I'm sorry about all this," Mason said.

Flushed and flustered, Effie looked at him, dazed. "It's OK. Wait—what do I owe you for the groceries?"

"Buy me lunch sometime," he said, and went out the door behind Iris. Neither of them spoke until they were in the elevator and the door had closed.

"You got it?" Iris asked.

"Yeah." He pulled the passport out of his pocket and swung his backpack off.

"He'll be thankful."

Reaching into his pants, Mason pulled out the cash bundles.

"Ew," Iris exclaimed.

"I didn't have many options."

"Are those hundreds? That's a lot of scratch to be keeping in your house. What does he do for a living?"

"I don't think I want to know," Mason said, dropping the bundles into his bag and swinging it back onto his shoulder. As they walked to the car, he said, "I appreciate your help. I couldn't have done it without you."

"I felt bad provoking her like that, and stirring things up, but it was the best way."

"I feel like a damn crook, lying to someone who trusts me, and breaking into her safe. It seems inexcusable."

"Well, the greater good is that you're helping Elmer get away from her. Next time she might use real bullets."

"There's that," Mason said grimly, pulling open the car door.

"Do you want a ride back to your bike?"

"That would be great. Do you know when visiting hours end at hospitals?"

"I think it's like eight or nine, so not yet," she said, backing the car out and flicking on the headlights.

"Good—I don't want to be carrying this around for very long."

"Why don't I just drop you there?" she said, pulling out onto the street.

"That's even better."

When she pulled up at the hospital, Mason climbed out and thanked her again.

"It was fun," she said, and grinned at him. "I'm sure I'll see you soon."

No one tried to slow him down on his way up to Elmer's room, although the nurse on duty in the ward gave him a reproachful beady-eyed once-over as he passed. Elmer was eating pudding out of a plastic cup and watching television. When Mason walked in, he sat up excitedly and killed the TV.

"Did you get it?"

"I did," he said, and slung off his backpack.

"Yes!" Elmer cackled, and pounded on the table, but quickly stopped, wincing with pain. "Don't pull it out right here," he said. "There's a bag in the little closet."

Mason went to the gym locker–size space beside

the door and looked inside, finding an empty black plastic shopping bag on a clothes hook.

"Sit down, and face me, so you're out of view if anyone walks in," Elmer instructed.

With the backpack in his lap, he put both hands inside and transferred the cash bundles and the passport into the plastic bag, then rolled it up, and glancing back at the doorway to make sure they were alone, passed it to Elmer.

Peeking into the bag, Elmer broke into a smile, then sighed and leaned back on his pillow. "I can't thank you enough," he said. "Can I give you a couple of C notes for your trouble?"

"No, man, it was a favor, not a job. I'm just glad you didn't ask me to bring your gun. I would have been nervous walking around with that."

"The nine mil?" he said, raising his eyebrows. "That's hers."

"Really?"

Elmer nodded, his expression somber. "She's got more going on than you'd think."

"Evidently," Mason said. "When do you get released?"

"They say tomorrow, which means I can skip out of here tonight."

"Where are you headed?"

"I'm not going to tell you, because you might tell her."

"Fair enough." Mason grinned, and sat forward in the chair. "I should go. Take care of yourself."

"I owe you one, bud."

Walking back to the café where his bike was, he felt lighter, relieved. He was done with both of them, he knew that now. Hanh said Effie's psychic disruption was resolved, and he'd done Elmer the favor he'd asked. He felt a twinge of guilt at violating Effie's trust, deceiving her like that in her own home. But Mason could disconnect now, put the whole thing behind him—and Detective Kerr could do his own damn work.

The café was still open, livelier with an evening crowd, and his bicycle was where he left it. He rode to the metro, and when he saw the train approaching, texted Ned:

Home in 90.

Ned soon replied, bringing a smile to his face as he stood in the cramped space with his wheels.

We'll eat when you get here.

By the time he got home, he'd come down from the intensity of the day, and felt emotionally drained. The dining table was set for dinner for three, and once he'd ditched his backpack and splashed some water on his face, Peggy set out a covered casserole dish and a big spoon.

"Simple tonight," she explained. "Shepherd's pie."

"Thanks for waiting," he said, sitting with her at the table.

"It's not that late," Ned said, joining them and

complimenting Peggy on the casserole. "It smells amazing."

Mason perked up a little once he had some food in his belly, and entertained them with his story about seeing Elmer, and visiting Effie, and rifling their safe.

Ned shook his head in amazement. "You're basically a burglar now. Do you realize that?"

"I was retrieving his stuff with his permission. That's not illegal."

"He told you the cash was his," Ned said, "but you don't really know that. It might have been hers."

Mason paused, setting his fork down. "I hadn't actually thought of that."

"At least the passport was his," Ned said. "You did check, didn't you?"

Mason just sighed.

"I hate that Effie and Iris were fighting over a man," Peggy said. "It's so lame."

"That was only the way it started—they were actually kind of arguing about mythology. Who was more tuned in to the allegory, and who was doing it better."

"Promise me you'll never go to their apartment again," Ned said, taking another scoop of shepherd's pie. "I'm afraid you'll get shot."

"Deal," he said. "And it's her place now. He's headed abroad."

"I was thinking about the name of the ship they were on, *The Pearl of Primordial Chaos*," Peggy said.

"Iris says it's from Chinese mythology."

"I was thinking your clients are like that: a whirl of primordial chaos."

Ned laughed. "How about 'a whirl of perpetual chaos'? It seems to be a sustained part of your life."

Mason nodded, considering that. "It's true, that's basically what my reality looks like. More important, I love that you're joking about it. It means you can handle it."

After dinner, Mason went into the office and spent some time making notes about his day, trying to remember how Iris had explained her ideas about archetypal stories and characters. When he'd torn the pages off his pad and slipped them into the case file, he picked up Ned's mythology book, reading more from Homer and Ovid until sleep overcame him.

The alarm went off early, and he stumbled out of bed, downing as much coffee as he could stomach and munching on some fruit. He had a standing appointment with his shrink, Miss Cassie, and she insisted on scheduling him early in the day. By the time he had dressed and pulled on his backpack, coasting down the hill on his bicycle, his resentment at being summoned so early was fading.

It was hard to be grumpy anyway, with a day of sunshine after yesterday's rainy winter weather, and he was still feeling buoyed by his success with Hanh and the decision to wind things up with the Brownsteins.

Miss Cassie's office was in a renovated art deco tower downtown, and coming up out of the metro across the street, he always felt inspired. He locked his wheels in a bicycle rack and rode up in the glammy mahogany-paneled elevator, sliding the sign on her office door from COME IN to PLEASE KNOCK before pushing it open. Miss Cassie waved from her desk. Today she was dressed in a sharp red jacket cut to deemphasize the weight on her frame. She was engrossed in a phone call, so he got comfortable in his usual seat, gazing out the tall windows overlooking the towers of the financial district.

"I love the light you get," he said, once she'd joined him.

"It's nice for a few hours," she said, folding open her tablet, "but it'll get dark way too soon. I hate this time of year."

"At least it's just a few weeks until it all turns around."

"The solstice?"

"It's the only time the Aegean is calm for a few days, thanks to Iris," he said.

Miss Cassie grinned. "You've been boning up on mythology? How germane is the temperament of the Aegean to your life?"

"It's actually pretty important. I've been dealing with people who are acting out similar stories, like echoes of mythological tales."

"In my business, we call them archetypes. Mythology resonates with modern people because it gives our own experiences deeper meaning."

"I'm so glad you think it's important," Mason said. "We don't usually see eye to eye on much."

"People in my trade use archetypes to shed light

on the workings of the subconscious. If you dream about a wizened old man trying to get your attention, what does that mean?"

"That seems open-minded of you, being a woman of the church."

"The modern monotheistic religions are toxic to human psychology," she said, meeting his gaze.

His eyebrows shot up. He couldn't believe he was hearing this from her. It sounded much more like something a nontheist would say—someone like Ned.

"In antiquity the gods squabbled," she continued, "but they never denied each other's existence. Today it's like you have an acre of land to grow food, and all you plant is one vegetable." She waved her hand. "Snap peas. That's not healthy. Monotheism impoverishes our creativity and our understanding of ourselves."

"Give me a second," Mason said, and reached down into his backpack to pull out his notepad, quickly writing down some of her ideas.

"Why are you reading about classical mythology?" she asked.

Mason told her about meeting Iris, and Effie and Elmer, and the reflections of classical allegory in their lives.

"Let's look at that," Cassie said, scribbling her own notes. "If you believe this woman is acting out Pomona's story, how does that impact your interaction with her?"

"It gives me another way to understand her. At

first I thought she was nuts, but I've revised that assessment. There's a lot of drama, and she's not especially stable, but she's actually pretty focused and functional."

"Good," Miss Cassie said, glancing up from her notes. "Then it's useful."

They talked about it for a while, and finally, setting aside her tablet, Miss Cassie said, "It was so nice to talk to you. You often bring something unexpected."

"I'm glad," Mason said, glancing at the wall clock and stuffing his notepad into his backpack.

"You know, Vertumnus said Pomona would be his last love."

"Meaning that he couldn't live without her?" Mason asked.

"Or maybe that he was destined to be with her. I wouldn't be surprised if Elmer and Effie get back together."

"I'm not sure that would be the healthiest option, given their track record," he said, rising from his chair. "But if nothing else, there's passion there."

Curious, Mason thought as he left, that Miss Cassie would have that kind of insight into people she'd never met. He slid her sign back to COME IN and headed down to the street.

fifteen

A couple of weeks later, after a leisurely breakfast with Ned on a chilly Saturday morning, Mason checked his email on his phone. There was a note from Iris.

> Please find a link below to stream the first cut of the episode of *America's Filthiest People* that you participated in. Keep in mind the final cut won't be broadcast for a couple of months.

"Do you want to see me do my psychic thing for a filthy person?" he asked Ned, who was putting their oatmeal dishes into the dishwasher.

"It's on TV already?"

"They sent me a link to the first draft."

"Tell Peggy," he said. "She's in her room, but she's awake. She won't want to miss this."

Ned spent a minute connecting his tablet to the TV set, and the three of them sat in the living room, Mason with Ned on the sofa. The episode began without the customary titles, launching right into a narration about Mary-Beth losing custody of her children because of her trash-filled home. Dr. Connie and Ray arrived and greeted Mary-Beth, walking into the house and staring around in wonder. Mason remembered watching them film that scene, but seeing it edited together, it all made much more sense. Mason's heart beat faster in anticipation as the narrator set up the next scene.

"One of the tragic losses in Mary-Beth's life was her beloved grandmother, who lived with Mary-Beth in the home until she died," he intoned. "Somewhere in the clutter is her grandmother's invaluable necklace." The video panned across the mountains of clutter, then cut to Mary-Beth.

"I've decided to hire a psychic to locate the necklace," she explained. "It would break my heart if that last keepsake from my grandmother got hauled away like it was garbage."

The video cut to Mason standing with Mary-Beth, explaining his technique. He'd seen video of himself before, but it was still startling to see how weird he looked, standing on the lawn at Mary-Beth's house, hands on his hips.

"Am I always that pasty?" he asked.

"It's just the lighting," Peggy said.

"It was broad daylight. Do I always slouch like that? You can't blame that on the light."

"It's just the camera angle," she said.

"You look fine," Ned said, and rewound the video a few seconds so they could hear what he was saying.

As he was talking on the screen, a subtitle appeared in a band at the bottom of the image:

Nelson Wrathway, psychic consultant

"Ouch," Peggy exclaimed.

Ned paused the feed. "That's the same misspelling they made on the TV news that time."

"I think I know what happened," Mason said slowly. "The postproduction guy recognized me from that story. He must have dug it up and copied my name from it."

"I'm sure there's still time to change it before it gets broadcast," Ned said.

"Maybe you don't have to," Peggy said. "Maybe it's a sign from the universe that you should have a stage name, or a TV name."

"Interesting," Mason said, considering the idea. "I could easily just create another online identity as Nelson Wrathway."

"It's actually a great idea," Ned said. "Keep your private life separate, and prevent the kooks from knocking on our door."

"My clients aren't kooks," Mason said, scowling at him.

"Not so far, but if they find you through *America's*

Filthiest People, they might be."

"Press Play," Mason said.

He hated watching himself, standing there on Mary-Beth's mountain of junk with his eyes screwed shut, reading the dog tags, but he couldn't look away; it was fascinating. When he mumbled "Not you, Percy," the camera zoomed in on his face. Watching it, seeing every freckle, Mason flinched. Thankfully it was only for a few seconds.

"As the day wore on," the narrator said, "tempers flared."

Standing outside her front door as a stream of trash bags was carted out behind her, Mary-Beth explained that she'd found the precious heirloom, no thanks to Mason, and when Dr. Connie admonished him, the image cut to a tight close-up of his face, red and sputtering.

"The crazy one is right behind you," he said to Dr. Connie. "Look inside her house." The camera stayed on him, his angry reaction caught in slow motion.

"Oh, my god," Mason said. "They make it look so dramatic. It wasn't anything like that."

Ned rewound a little to watch the scene again, not concealing his amusement.

"I'm sorry, but that necklace is no precious heirloom," Ned said. "It looks like something a cartoon character would wear."

"I know, right?" Mason said emphatically.

Peggy laughed. "I can't believe you damaged her precious stuff with your mind, you bastard."

"You can see how precious it all is," Mason said. "Those empty potato-chip cans are probably worth a fortune."

They watched the cleanup continue, and Ray screaming at Mary-Beth about her babies. The image cut to Mason again, sitting far off under a tree, his arms draped around his knees. Ray walked over, and he jumped up to greet him.

"Oh, no," Mason said, feeling the blood rush to his head. "No, no, no …"

"What's wrong?" Ned said, pausing the video.

"We can stop watching now. It's basically over."

"No freaking way," Peggy said. "You're blushing. That means it's going to get good."

Most of their conversation had been edited out, up to the point where Ray said, "Do you want to make out?"

"Whoa," Ned said, sitting forward. "Get your greasy mitts off my man."

Ned watched intently as the conversation played out. At the end of the scene, after Mason had rejected him, Ray said, "I respect your integrity, Mason," and walked away.

Mason sat back, stunned. "They changed that. What he really said was that I was missing out. They must have dubbed it in later."

"It does make for compelling viewing," Peggy said. "Ray looks so confident and seductive. Plus he respects your integrity. That's a sign of character."

"But it's not what he really said."

"For the viewer, though, Ray comes off as

completely well-mannered," she said.

"I can't believe they put that in. I didn't know they were filming us."

"You knew you were wearing a mike," Ned said. "You didn't think they'd use that scene? It's so juicy."

"I guess I'm surprised because Ray never hit on anyone before."

"This must be his coming-out episode," Ned said. "I always thought he seemed kind of gay."

"You, mister, should be thrilled that Mason reacted that way," Peggy said. "He totally could have macked on that guy."

"You're right," Ned said. "I am glad." He took Mason's hand and kissed the back of it. "Thank you for not sleeping with other people."

They watched the rest of the episode, cringing at Mary-Beth's filth and laughing heartily at Mason's final reaction to the clean house.

"You'd think you'd never seen a clean carpet before," Ned said.

"Let's not tell anyone about this," Mason said when it was over. "If any of our friends see it, so be it. But let's not advertise."

"Are you kidding?" Peggy said. "I'm going to blast an email announcement to everyone I've ever met. We're having a viewing party here, or maybe we'll even rent a ballroom at the Baltimore."

Mason knew it was inevitable that people would see it—that had been part of the deal from the start, and it wasn't even really that embarrassing, but still, it made him feel queasy. He went out onto the balcony, still chilly in the shadows of the low winter sun, to take a breath. The chair felt cold through his sweatpants, but it wouldn't hurt for a minute or two, and it was helping calm his stomach. His phone buzzed in his pocket, and when he pulled it out, he saw that it was a video call request. He didn't recognize the user name but answered anyway.

In the video frame he saw Elmer, who smiled when he saw Mason.

"Hey, buddy, how're you doing?" Elmer said. He panned the camera slightly to the side, and Effie leaned into the frame.

"Look at you two," Mason said, stunned that they were back together.

"You look kind of pale, Mason," Effie said, grinning and waving.

"That's genetic. Where are you?" Mason asked. "It looks really bright there."

"Puerto Vallarta, sucker," Elmer said, and panned the camera to one side, revealing the green-blue ocean stretching to the horizon. "We're on the fourteenth floor. Private patio, full ocean view."

"Nice."

"There's a nightclub on the first floor, though," he said, grimacing slightly, "so it's a bit loud."

Effie crowded back into the frame. "We wanted to thank you for helping us get here."

"What are you talking about? I had no idea that you were going down there." Or that you were getting back together, he thought.

"If you hadn't taken Elmer's passport and cash,"

she said, "he wouldn't have been able to scope out an apartment for us."

Mason felt his cheeks redden, and he self-consciously straightened the phone, glancing at the tiny image of himself. "I felt bad about doing that right under your nose, and having Iris start a fight."

She nodded. "I can handle anything that twerp has to say. That was pretty naughty of you, sneaking into the safe without telling me. But I know you had a good reason, and you were under orders from my shnuggle bunny."

"So are you living there now?"

"Just for a couple of months," Elmer said, turning the camera toward himself. "We'll come home in the spring. The weather is so nice here, and the food—you'd love it."

"Ooh, look!" Effie cried, and grabbed for the camera, twisting it around until Mason was looking at a jiggling blue-green seascape. A string of blurry brown blobs sailed by.

"Birds?" Mason asked.

"Pelicans," Effie said. "There are tons of them here. They patrol up and down the beach." She twisted the camera back to the two of them, and leaned close to Elmer, almost cheek to cheek, the two of them smiling.

"We won't keep you. We just wanted to say hello and let you know we're both doing well," Elmer said.

"Right. Well, it was good to see you," Mason said. "Have fun down there."

They waved good-bye and the call disconnected.

Mason chuckled and spoke again to the empty screen. "And don't kill each other."

Also from Dagmar Miura

The Mason Braithwaite Paranormal Mystery Series

In the previous books in the series, no one is ever quite sure whether psychic investigator Mason gets results with actual psychic power or his more mundane flatfooting, but the disheveled redhead manages to resolve some intractable mysteries.

mason.dagmarmiura.com

The Slater Ibáñez Books

Don't mess with the hothead—or he might just mess with you. Slater is only interested in two kinds of guys: the ones he wants to punch, and the ones he sleeps with. Things get interesting when they start to overlap.

slater.dagmarmiura.com

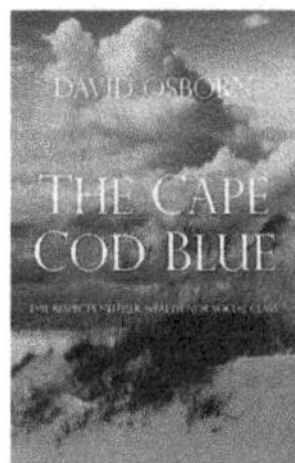

The Cape Cod Blue

The glittering, exalted world of art auctioning hides love, hate, and parricidal murder in a wealthy and socially prominent family when forgery of an anonymous Cape Cod painting is used to steal a world-famous portrait that's worth a fortune.

capecod.dagmarmiura.com

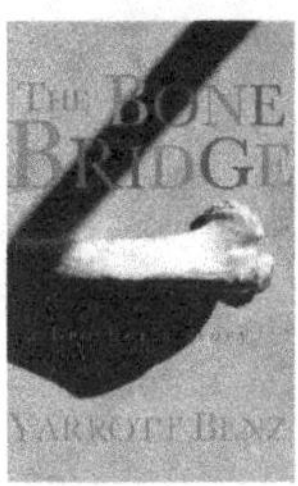

The Bone Bridge

Yarrott Benz, the 2016 Ippy Award winner for memoir, is forced to deal with extraordinary self-sacrifice in this harrowing account of teenage brothers, as different as night and day, trapped together in a dramatic medical dilemma.

bonebridge.dagmarmiura.com